The crime was doggone sinister. Soon, the police would be barking up the wrong tree.

All at once, a man popped up in front of me. It was the big ruddy-faced man Eugene had fought with earlier. His face was now pale as he tried to speak, but he gasped for air instead.

Thinking perhaps he had claustrophobia or was having a panic attack of some sort, I laid my hand on his arm and asked, "Are you okay? What's wrong?"

He opened his mouth, but still nothing.

The man reached out to me and grabbed my shoulder. I winced as his hand leaned on Grandma Tillie's brooch and pushed it into my flesh. He lunged forward against me, knocking me off balance.

"Sir? Sir, what's the problem?"

As he fell at my feet, my question was answered.

The problem was there was a very large carving knife sticking out of his back.

———

"Catnip for mystery fans!"
—*Maggie, the cat of Donald Bain (MURDER SHE WROTE SERIES)*

The Pampered Pets Mysteries from Bell Bridge Books

Desperate Housedogs

Get Fluffy

Kitty Kitty Bang Bang

Yip/Tuck

Fifty Shades of Greyhound

The Girl with the Dachshund Tattoo
(Fall, 2014)

Fifty Shades of Greyhound

by

Sparkle Abbey

Bell Bridge Books

This is a work of fiction. Names, characters, places and incidents are either the products of the author's imagination or are used fictitiously. Any resemblance to actual persons (living or dead), events or locations is entirely coincidental.

Bell Bridge Books
PO BOX 300921
Memphis, TN 38130
Print ISBN: 978-1-61194-418-1

Bell Bridge Books is an Imprint of BelleBooks, Inc.

We at BelleBooks enjoy hearing from readers.
Visit our websites
BelleBooks.com
BellBridgeBooks.com
ImaJinnBooks.com

10 9 8 7 6 5 4 3 2 1

Cover design: Debra Dixon
Interior design: Hank Smith
Photo/Art credits:
Girl (manipulated) © Aleutie | Dreamstime.com
Dog (manipulated) © Dawn Hudson | Dreamstime.com
Collar © Roughcollie | Dreamstime.com
Paw print © Booka1 | Dreamstime.com

:Lsfg:01:

Dedication

To all the animal rescue groups, the staff and the volunteers, who not only love animals but put that love into action with hard work and dedication.

Chapter One

IT WAS A KILLER party.

Blanche LeRue, CEO of Greys Matter, barked orders for more seating, more native California bubbly, and more gourmet shrimp appetizers. I'm sure Blanche hoped the overflow crowd translated to big donations for the Greyhound rescue.

Her dress was a formal length charcoal satin that complemented her tall, reed-like figure. A commanding woman, she wore her chin-length silver hair in a way that framed her narrow face yet still managed to look more regal than severe. But make no mistake, Blanche LeRue was a regal with a cause. And that cause was Greyhound rescue.

I know it must seem to y'all that I'm always at some big fancy schmancy party. You've probably also noted that it's usually an animal-related fancy schmancy deal. You'd be right. That's me, Caro Lamont, pet therapist and big-time subscriber to the there-are-no- bad-pets-just-uneducated-pet-parents philosophy.

My Laguna Beach pet therapy business is called PAWS, which stands for Professional Animal Wellness Specialist, but, in truth, I work more with problem people than problem pets.

Invitations to charity events abound in this pet-friendly southern California haven, but tonight's gala was a special one, the Fifty Shades of Greyhound Charity Ball, at *D'Orange Maison*, a gorgeous historic ranch estate just outside of Laguna Beach. The main house had recently been spiffed up, the huge rooms used for wedding receptions, political affairs, celebrity functions, and events such as this five-thousand-dollar-a-ticket fund-raiser.

The room was shades of gray everywhere. Pale gray skirting and deep gray brocade tablecloths, slate-colored vases filled with silver floral arrangements.

I know what you're thinking: they were playing off the mega success of a book that started with the same phrase. Well, you'd probably be right, but you have to admit it was for a great cause. And there were truly fifty, count them, *fifty* real live Greyhounds of varying shades staged at strategic places around the room. Most sat at attention at the feet of their owners or handlers. Though all the dogs were not gray—some white, some black, and still others fawn or brindle—all were adorned with gray leather collars. Blanche LeRue was nothing if not a detail person.

There were many wonderful Greyhound rescue groups in California, but Greys Matter was, in my opinion, one of the best. I hoped the clink and clatter of the crystal and china as waiters refilled champagne glasses and people filled their plates was echoed by the *cha-ching* of hefty contributions to the rescue group.

Speaking of details, Blanche and her event committee had come up with the idea of silver-framed signs around the room printed with factoids about Greyhounds. It was a superb idea. What a great way to convey important information to attendees without some talking head standing at a microphone. I'd seen it time and time again—people who'd paid a pricey admission impatiently waiting for a speaker to be done so they could resume their conversations. People were still waiting, but they were waiting in line to pile gourmet food on their china. And the Greys Matter crew had made sure the buffet tables were placed strategically close to the framed signs. Brilliant.

Part of the fun of attending events like this one was the people-watching. There's always more to people than what you first noticed. Ever a student of human behavior, I loved the opportunity to observe.

Which was why I stood watching people while Sam Gallanos, my—well heck, what was Sam?

My friend? No, we're more than friends. My lover? No, less than that one? My escort? Now that just sounds wrong, doesn't it? My man? My main squeeze? Hmmm. What we were to each other was complicated. So for now, let's just call him my date for the evening.

Sam, my "date" was off fighting the crowd for a plate of food. While I enjoyed the people-watching, I hoped he'd be back soon. Partly because I enjoyed his fabulous company, and partly because I'd begun to get hungry.

I looked around the spectacular ballroom. Several of my PAWS clients were in attendance. I spotted retired news tycoon Davis Pinter standing near a sign that said, "The origin of the Greyhound name has nothing to do with color. In fact, gray is not a common color among Greyhounds." That was true.

Davis is a lovely man, always well-dressed, and he looked snappy tonight in his gray tux. Davis has an adorable Cavalier King Charles

Spaniel named Huntley. A smart man and a smart dog, but sometimes there ensued a battle of wills between the two, which was how we'd become acquainted.

Each of the signs had an artistic outline of a Greyhound at the top. The one closest to me said, "Before the 1980s, many racing Greyhounds were put down at the end of their careers. Now, thanks to rescue groups like Greys Matter, more than 20,000 are adopted each year."

I knew the stats, but still seeing them in black and white was sobering. I could understand why Blanche and the other volunteers were so passionate about Greyhound rescue.

I saw my friend, Diana Knight, across the way and a smile welled up inside me. Her elegant, perfectly-coiffed, blond head bobbed up and down as she talked. She'd cornered a California congressman near another sign which stated, "Most Greyhounds are at the end of their racing careers at two to five years of age, but they still have a lot of life to live. The average lifespan is twelve to fourteen years." Diana pointed at the words on the sign and pointed at the congressman.

What Diana Knight is to me isn't at all complicated. Diana is my very best friend in the world. She's eighty-something and old-school Hollywood at its best, having starred in a number of golden age romantic comedies as the perky heroine who always got the best of the guy.

Well, perky had morphed into feisty. Based on the distance of her perfectly manicured finger from said congressman's nose, Diana was definitely getting the best of the politician. I couldn't hear the conversation because of all the chatter in the room, but I was willing to bet it had something to do with animal rights. With Diana it was always about the animals. You always knew where you stood with her and she unapologetically lived her passion. I aspired to be Diana Knight when I grew up.

Diana was dressed in gray like the rest of us, though her dress was a soft, silvery-gray chiffon, the perfect foil for her delicate coloring. I knew she'd want to do lunch soon so we could dish on who was with whom, and which designers made the best show.

The main door opened and the last few arrivals hurried inside, victims of a steady rainfall. We could use the rain, but maybe *D'Orange Maison* should think about a covered portico.

Tova Randall sashayed into the ballroom with the new man in her life. I'd heard she'd been out of the country. Tonight, all eyes were on her as she made an entrance in a gray-toned sheath that hugged her silicone-enhanced curves. Tova was sprinkled with raindrops which looked good on her flawless skin. She'd been a very successful lingerie model and, on her, the rain almost looked like an accessory in a photo shoot. I was thankful I'd arrived before the rain as the moisture would not have been as kind to my naturally-curly red locks.

Tova's previous significant-other relationship had met with an unfortunate end. I'd not been much of a fan of the woman, but no one deserved what she'd been through. I was glad to see Tova was getting out.

My cousin, Melinda Langston, who owned the Bow Wow Boutique, an über-fancy pet shop in downtown Laguna Beach, had been involved in solving the murder of Tova's boyfriend and plastic surgeon, Dr. O'Doggle.

Speaking of Melinda—where was she?

I scanned the room of high-steppers. They were all tricked out in gray and black and silver fashions, but dark-haired Mel with her striking good looks would be easy to spot. I didn't see her.

It wasn't like her to miss a rescue event. I'd heard she and Grey Donovan, local art gallery owner and her on-again-off-again fiancé, had been seen around town. So the current future wedding status must be "on." I think it was a sure bet I could count myself out as a bridesmaid.

Mel's mama and my mama were sisters. We'd been childhood best friends, even up through our teen years and into our twenties. We shared a background of over-achieving high-competition mothers. We shared a love of critters. We shared a loathing of the pageant circuit.

But then things had happened, words were said, and, well, it's beyond complicated and partly involves the brooch I wore tonight.

You see, our Grandma Tillie had left the bejeweled basket of fruit pin to her "favorite granddaughter." She only had two granddaughters. Clearly, only one could be the favorite. That would be me. I'd recently retrieved the brooch from Mel's possession and I sure as shootin' did not want her to miss seeing me wear it tonight.

"Hello, Caro." Alana Benda appeared at my side. "Isn't this awesome?" Her voice was a little too bright. A little too loud. Either too much excitement or her champagne glass had been refilled a few too many times.

"It is," I agreed. "A great turnout, and the venue is absolutely stunning."

"Speaking of stunning, is your dress a Jenny Packman?" Alana tapped the peplum skirt of my silver-gray satin gown, her heavy diamond tennis bracelet winking in the lights.

"It is." I could have worn something I had, but I didn't really own anything formal in gray. Not a great color for a redhead. Besides, why pass up an excuse to buy a new dress? Right? Especially something from the newest hot designer. I loved the simplicity of her designs, although I'd worried the delicate beading would be damaged by the brooch prominently pinned to my left shoulder.

"I thought so." Alana looked like she thought there might be a prize involved for the correct guess.

Also, I got the impression I'd suddenly been raised a few notches in her who-might-possibly-be-important list. Leave it to Alana to be into the haute couture label on what everyone was wearing. Not that Diana and I wouldn't be doing a designer debrief when we got together for lunch, but we weren't picking our friends based the status on their closet.

Alana had picked a silver and black Roberto Cavalli animal print that accented her toned-to-the-max body. I didn't know Alana all that well except for talking to her at functions like this.

She was married to Dave, the accountant who had an office in the group where PAWS was located, but come to think of it, I didn't really know Dave that well either. He wasn't around the place a lot and when he was, it seemed he was always busy. During tax season, there was a steady stream of wealthy Laguna residents coming through the office. I imagined the guy needed to work long hours if his wife had a penchant for designer dresses and diamond bracelets.

I glanced over Alana's shoulder at the silver-framed placard behind her. "Greyhounds are bred and built for speed but they are often referred to as 40 MPH couch potatoes. They are exceptionally calm dogs."

That was true. Greyhounds were great family dogs. Gentle and good-natured.

I clearly didn't know much about Dave because I hadn't realized he and his wife were interested in Greyhound rescue.

"Do you and Dave have Greyhounds?" It didn't necessarily follow, though many attendees at the event did.

"We do." She flipped bleached blond bangs out of her eyes. "We have two Italian Greyhounds, Louie and Lexie."

Italian Greyhounds are extremely slender and the smallest of the sighthounds. They looked like miniature Greyhounds, but a lot of IG owners didn't care for the term. The American Kennel Club sees them as true genetic Greyhounds, with a bloodline going back more than two thousand years.

The main thing as far as my PAWS clients go is, while they're incredibly sweet and well-behaved, an Italian Greyhound, like any Greyhound, should not be trusted off leash because they have an extremely high predator drive. That means, you may be walking with your dog and suddenly he takes off after a small animal. Not good at the dog park.

"They're great dogs." I waited, expecting her to pull out pictures of her fur kids, or point them out if they were in the room. Most of the pet owners I'd talked to did once the topic came up.

Not Alana.

Her fake eyelashes fluttered. "And David is the CFO for Greys Matter." She gestured with her champagne glass toward the corner of the room where Dave stood talking to Alice Tiburon and her husband, Robert.

I knew CFO meant Chief Financial Officer, but Alana's tone implied it meant Dave and Warren Buffett were pals.

I glanced over at the trio. Alice Tiburon was the chair of the board of Greys Matter and she definitely was no trophy wife. In fact, she was the one with the money in that pairing. She was a very successful businesswoman. The Tiburons had recently moved from their mansion in Ruby Point to a bigger mansion in the even more exclusive gated community of Diamond Cove. On the coast, and in Laguna in particular, it's all about the view, and this Diamond Cove property was purported to have the best view in Orange County. Certainly it was one of the most expensive.

Dave and Robert wore gray tuxes like the rest of the men. Alice was striking in a gray crepe ribbon-striped gown that perfectly accented her slender height and her shoulder-length dark hair. I wondered if Alana had asked her who the designer was.

I should say hello to Dave and the couple. I'd known the Tiburons had Greyhounds, but apparently not problem ones. Or, if so, they used a different pet therapist. Alice and Robert Tiburon were regulars at Laguna Beach events and a solid supporter of pet causes. I knew the latter because she was often on Diana's donor list.

I turned back to speak to Alana, but she had moved away, obviously spotting another potentially important person in designer dress. I looked around once again for Sam, and my glance caught Blanche LeRue's silver head as she surveyed the crowd and the lavishly decorated *D'Orange Maison* ballroom. I could see a slight frown form as she noted the gaps in the sumptuous platters of food surrounding the towering Greyhound dog ice sculpture.

She waved over Dino Riccio. The dapper Italian caterer hurried to her side and, in turn, motioned to Eugene, the latest addition to his catering team. Dino owned the popular Riccio's Italian restaurant and was also the current leading man in Diana Knight's life.

Eugene, the new foodie recruit, was the twin brother of Verdi, an über multitasker who'd we'd recently hired as a part-time receptionist for our shared office group. She'd been recruited after an unfortunate series of ill-suited temps.

Scanning the room again, I finally spotted Sam making his way toward me through the crowd with two plates of food. Thank heavens! I was famished.

He caught my attention, and I felt a little answering kick in my gut from the warmth of his gaze across the distance.

Even in this crush of people, the guy stood out. It hardly seemed fair. It was a gray-tie affair so it was a level playing field. Every man in the room was pretty much dressed the same, yet still, Sam's air of relaxed assurance along with his Greek heritage added up to something that turned heads. At least female ones. Call it charisma or sex appeal or whatever you want, Sam had it in spades.

There was a sudden break in the chatter around me and I turned away from the sight of Sam and my food to see what had drawn everyone's attention. There was some sort of a commotion over by the room's service door.

I stood on tiptoes to see over heads. No small feat, let me tell you, in my new silver-strappy Jimmy Choos. Eugene and one of the guests were in a heated exchange. There was a collective gasp as one of the Greyhound signs fell into a stack of used silverware which hit the floor with a clatter. Both men were red-faced.

I'd vouched for Eugene to Dino, who'd needed extra help for the party, but I knew him only in passing. I knew Verdi and I'd figured if they were related, he had some of her work ethic and multitasking skills. And Dino had been in a tight spot.

I hoped Eugene hadn't spilled something on the guy.

The man was bigger and towered over Eugene, but the young man did not back down. At least his body language said so. Finally with a shove to Eugene's shoulder, the ruddy-faced fellow stalked off and Eugene continued through the service door.

After a slight pause, we all went back to our conversations. I worried about the argument and if there'd been damage, but not overly. According to Dino, there are always mishaps and disgruntled guests at every function. Dino was a pro—he'd sort things out.

I'd turned to look for Sam and those plates of food, when Blanche suddenly appeared beside me. I'm tall, but the woman had to be at least six feet, and she practically vibrated with energy. She was in her element and having the time of her life.

"Hi, hon, how's the event going?" I asked.

"Great. Just great." Blanche's blue eyes snapped with excitement. "I think we'll hit our goal before the night is over."

"Everything looks wonderful. The signs were a brilliant idea. And I can't believe the ice sculpture of the Greyhound." I pointed toward the banquet table. "And the rabbit looks so lifelike."

"Rabbit?" She frowned and turned toward the table. "There's no—"

Just then the rabbit moved.

"Well, for cryin' in a bucket." The rabbit looked like a real bunny rabbit because it *was* a real bunny.

The furry floppy-eared critter scampered the length of the loaded feast, honey-glazed carrot clamped in its teeth, leaving a trail of shrimp cocktail bunny tracks across the buffet. Then the rabbit went airborne onto the closest guest table.

Which was all it took. It was like the starting gun had been fired.

The Greyhound stationed near the table sighted the hare and began the chase. Instantly, chaos reigned.

Hound chased rabbit, hound chased hound, humans chased hounds. Leashes trailed, tables tipped, trays of glasses tumbled.

I could still see Sam, but he was carried backward by the wave of people and Greyhounds. Complete and utter pandemonium.

I surveyed the bedlam to see what I could do to help.

I decided one Greyhound at a time was the best tactic. I started toward the closest dog, a beautiful jet-black hound.

All at once, a man popped up in front of me. It was the big ruddy-faced man Eugene had fought with earlier. His face was now pale as he tried to speak, but he gasped for air instead.

Thinking perhaps he had claustrophobia or was having a panic attack of some sort, I laid my hand on his arm and asked, "Are you okay? What's wrong?"

He opened his mouth, but still nothing.

The man reached out to me and grabbed my shoulder. I winced as his hand leaned on Grandma Tillie's brooch and pushed it into my flesh. He lunged forward against me knocking me off balance.

"Sir? Sir, what's the problem?"

As he fell at my feet, my question was answered.

The problem was there was a very large carving knife sticking out of his back.

Chapter Two

THE CROWD PARTED around us like the Red Sea.

I was tempted to yell out, "Is there a doctor in the house?" But I knew the answer. There were no medical doctors on the guest list. However, before I yelled anything, Dr. Daniel Darling, Laguna Beach's premier veterinarian, hurried along the cleared marble-floor path to my side.

He handed me his cell phone and said, "Call 911." Then he knelt beside the man and laid a finger against his neck.

I made the call, quickly explaining the situation and giving the location. The room was still mass confusion as all the dogs had not yet been rounded up. I could hear Blanche calling out to various helpers to take the dogs to an adjoining room so they could be matched up with their owners. The whole situation was out of control.

I stayed by the prone man with Dr. Darling, but I felt useless.

"Isn't there something we can do?"

Dr. Darling shook his head.

It seemed like forever before the ambulance arrived, but I'm sure it was only a matter of minutes. The paramedics moved onlookers out of the way and dropped their equipment beside the man. I could see from Dr. Darling's face, though, that it was too late.

Sam helped me up from where I'd been crouched on the floor. "Caro?" His dark eyes searched my face.

"I'm okay." My hand shook as he held it, but, yeah, I was okay.

We moved out of the way so the paramedics could do their job.

Homicide Detective Judd Malone must have been nearby, because he arrived with a team of crime scene techs even before the paramedics had packed up their bags.

We were all herded to one side of the room and sorted into groups. Then, one by one, people were taken to another room for questioning. Poor Blanche was beside herself at that point. She paced back and forth. At least the police allowed Dino's crew to serve water to the stunned guests.

This was not how people who pay five thousand dollars a ticket expected to be treated.

One tall thin man, his gray bow tie in hand, simply got up and headed out the door.

A young uniformed officer halted him. "I'm sorry, sir, you're not cleared to leave."

As the uniform stepped in front of the fleeing guest, I realized it was Officer Hostas whom I knew from a little broken taillight incident a while back.

"You can't stop me," the thin man snapped, his face pinched, his look disgusted, like he'd discovered he'd stepped in doggie doo.

They were at a standoff, like two prizefighters sizing each other up. Blanche stood by wringing her hands. My money was on Officer Hostas.

"I can arrest you." Hostas looked like he thought that would be exciting. Without breaking eye contact, he shifted his hand to the police baton on his belt.

The errant guest sat back down. And the rest of us decided we would wait until we were cleared to leave. Whenever that might be.

They were doing the interviews in an adjoining banquet room and it seemed they'd broken us into three groups: those who were oblivious to what had happened, those who'd been running around chasing Greyhounds when the incident occurred, and those of us who were in the immediate vicinity when the man collapsed.

The oblivious group had been questioned first. Sam and Diana were in the second group as they'd been trying to help round up the dogs. I was, unfortunately, in the third and final group.

People were dismissed after they were questioned, and Blanche apologized profusely to each of the exiting patrons. The rest of us, who'd not yet been interviewed, sat on chairs we'd pulled up and talked about the evening's events. I know it seems callous, but people handle shock in different ways.

I settled in to wait for my turn, only half-listening to the chatter. I tucked my silver-gray gown around my knees. I felt a little shaky, a little chilled, but mostly kind of out of it.

The conversations eddied around me.

I caught a gruff-voiced complaint from a man who fussed with whoever would listen that the police could not hold "innocent people hostage."

Alana's petulant voice came through, detailing who she'd been talking to and what designer they were wearing, and she didn't know why she had to stay because she didn't even see the man.

Finally, Alice Tiburon's deep contralto answered with a "Would you *please* shut up?" which seemed to quiet Alana for a while.

Also, I wasn't sure who first said it, but there was a buzz that one of the waiters had gone missing.

Alice said, "I saw the young man who'd argued with the dead man go outside and then I saw the man come in. So they'd been outside together."

That got my attention. Eugene had been outside with the victim? I was in the same area but hadn't noticed the two of them after the confrontation. Of course, I'd been pretty focused on Sam and those plates of food.

The ambience of an elegant fête had turned to post-apocalyptic cleanup as a crew picked up broken furniture and glass. A medical person checked folks for injuries, which thankfully appeared to be minor. The room was warm. I reached up to feel my cheeks and as I raised my hands I suddenly realized my brooch was gone.

I shot out of my seat and dashed over to where the CSI techs were gathering evidence. Where the man's body lay, thankfully covered. I looked around on the floor and finally got down on my hands and knees.

"What do you think you're doing?"

I knew that voice. Detective Judd Malone.

I looked up, still on my hands and knees, not willing to give up the search. He stood, arms crossed, typical Malone stance.

"I'm trying to find a piece of jewelry." I hitched up my fancy gray dress and stood, teetering on silver-toned heels that'd seemed a good idea hours ago.

Malone reached out a hand to steady me. Like I mentioned before, I'm tall. Detective Malone is one of the few people who manages to make me feel petite. The unsmiling expression on his handsome face told me I was in for it.

"Why me?" He looked away and then looked back, pinning me with his hard blue gaze. "Tell me, what does your jewelry have to do with my crime scene?"

"The man," I pointed to the sheet-covered body. "When he talked to me, he grabbed my shoulder and must have dislodged my brooch."

"It's that brooch, isn't it?" he asked.

"What?"

"It's the family brooch, right?"

"Well, yes." I met his steely gaze. "Of course it is."

"Was your cousin, Mel, here to see it?"

"No, she wasn't." I jammed my hair behind my ears.

"What a shame." His expression said he didn't mean it.

He turned to the crime scene tech who was painstakingly examining the area. "Did you see a piece of jewelry?"

"No," the young man answered. "I didn't."

"There you have it." Malone wiped a hand over his face. "You must have lost it somewhere else."

"Could it . . . ?" I swallowed. "Could it be under . . . you know . . . him?" I pointed at the dead guy.

Malone motioned another tech over and the two of them lifted the man slightly.

Nothing.

"See, no brooch?" Malone shrugged. "I don't know what to tell you."

But when they'd moved the body, I could see the man's right hand, and sure enough, there it was, clutched in his curled fingers. He must have held onto it when he grabbed me and then fell.

"Um, Detective?" I pointed at the brooch.

"Well, what do you know?" The crime scene tech touched the pin with his tweezers.

I wanted to tell him to be careful with the heirloom piece, but I knew I was already on thin ice with Malone. And I've always been told you should never venture on thin ice with a fancy skater.

"Okay, Caro." Detective Malone put his hands on my shoulders and turned me back toward the chairs where the other witnesses sat waiting.

"But my—" I pointed to my brooch.

"Not now." He was out of patience. "Right now, I need you to go sit down with the others. We'll sort this out and we'll talk to everyone as quickly as we can."

"Of course." It *was* a crime scene after all.

I went back and sat down and, true to his word, it wasn't long before it was my turn to be questioned.

The uniformed officers who'd been taking guests' names and contact information took mine, although I was pretty sure the Laguna Beach Homicide Division had me on file. There'd been a couple of cases in the not-too-distant past where I'd been involved, much to

Malone's chagrin, in the crime-solving.

Malone asked me to describe what I'd seen and what exactly the man had said to me. I explained he hadn't been able to speak and recounted what I could remember of what had transpired.

"Did you know the victim?"

"No, I don't think I'd ever met him before tonight."

"Did you see him interact with other people throughout the evening?"

I hesitated. He'd had words with Eugene. What had looked like angry words. But I was sure there was a simple explanation for the exchange. Eugene would be able to clear it up. Perhaps the man had been unhappy with his food. Or maybe, as I'd thought at the time, Eugene had spilled something on him.

"Yes, I did see him talking with Eugene Perry," I finally said. "They both appeared to be somewhat upset."

"Really?" Malone stared me down. He waited silently. I knew it was a technique used to make people uncomfortable with the silence so they would talk. I had used it in counseling sessions back when I was a therapist to people, before my switch to four-legged clients. It seemed the police also used it in interrogation.

"Yes." I kept my answer simple.

"Several people described it as a very heated exchange and said this waiter, Eugene, shoved the man."

I shook my head. "It was the other way around. The man pushed Eugene's shoulder." I demonstrated on Malone.

He didn't move. His leather jacket was soft but there was nothing soft about the muscle underneath.

I pulled my hand back. "Whatever happened, I'm sure Eugene can clear things up."

"That's part of our problem, Caro. This waiter, Eugene, is missing and the carving knife in the man's back is the one from the buffet table where he was working. Do you know him?"

"Eugene is Verdi's brother." I explained. "You know, the barista from the Koffee Klatch. She's also our new receptionist at the office."

"Well then, you'd better give me your receptionist's phone number because her brother has a lot of explaining to do."

I reached in my evening bag for my cell phone and read off the number to Malone. He wrote it down.

"Hopefully, he's been in touch with her and we can pick him up quickly."

"I'm sure there's a reason he left."

"For his sake, I hope so." Malone stood. "But it doesn't look good."

I also stood and moved to leave. "Are you done with me?"

"For now."

I started toward the door and then remembered and turned back. Malone was already mid-dial on his cell. Probably calling Verdi.

"Detective, my brooch?"

"Can't give it to you, Caro. It's evidence."

"What do you mean, it's evidence?"

"Found in the victim's hand. Evidence."

"But you know it's mine."

I was sorry for the dead guy, really I was. But the idea that Grandma Tillie's brooch had anything to do with why he was dead was beyond belief.

"It will probably be released in a short time, but for the time being, it stays in police evidence." Malone went back to his phone.

There wasn't a thing I could do, and I guess it was as safe a place as any. But seriously, evidence?

No doubt Grandma Matilda "Tillie" Montgomery was rolling over in her grave.

IT WAS A SHORT trip from *D'Orange Maison* back to Laguna and to my house. Sam let the silence lay between us on the drive. He seemed to know I needed the quiet time. In addition to being the most eligible A-list bachelor, the charming Greek was also a genuinely nice guy. An irresistible combination.

As soon as I was inside, I slipped out of my gray frock and hung it in the front of my closet so I'd remember to take it to the cleaners. I was exhausted, but sleep did not come easily.

I kept thinking about the man who'd been stabbed at the Fifty Shades of Greyhound Charity Ball. I'd seen dead people before, but I'd never had one die right in front of me.

Who was this man? I knew a lot of people in Laguna, but I didn't think I'd met him prior to the event.

And then there was Eugene, Verdi's brother, who had seemed like a safe bet. He'd argued with the man, and then the man had shown up with a carving knife in his back. People had seen them both come in from outside. Maybe Eugene had nothing to do with the stabbing but, if not, why had he immediately disappeared?

And poor Blanche LeRue and the Greys Matter rescue. What a disastrous ending to the evening. The group would survive, according to Diana, but they'd really been banking on this event being a huge success.

Chapter Three

THE MEDIA CALLED it "The Carving Knife Murder."

Malone and crew had questioned every single person at the Greyhound event. It seemed there were just short of a hundred witnesses, and yet no one had actually seen the man get stabbed. I knew they'd needed to ask the questions when details were fresh in all of our minds, but I also knew eyewitness accounts were often unreliable. By the time I'd finally fallen asleep last night, I wasn't sure myself about what I'd seen. And yet this morning, I felt like parts of the incident were burned into my memory.

According to the news report, the victim was new to the area and, while he'd been photographed at several recent Laguna Beach pet and marine life rescue events, they could find no one to interview who actually knew him.

The news anchor called him a wealthy Orange County business man. And I guess he would have to have been, to attend a big dollar function like the Fifty Shades of Greyhound charity event.

Poor Blanche. This was not good news coverage for Greys Matter. Last night, she had been a wreck. The in-charge Blanche had been replaced by a harried woman whose classy event was in ruins. The bad publicity would take some major PR damage control.

And I didn't think *D'Orange Maison* would be returning her deposit anytime soon, given the breakage caused by the dogs and the people attempting to round up the dogs. What a mess.

I had tried to reach Verdi first thing this morning. I tried again while my coffee brewed, but her cell phone went directly to voicemail. Malone had undoubtedly called her last night. I knew he had to, but I felt a bit like a traitor not having the chance to tell her what had happened before the police called. In the light of day, I was sure there was a good reason Eugene had disappeared from the event.

I'd try to catch Verdi at the office before I began the day's pet appointments.

I showered and threw on my well-worn Rag and Bone jeans and a

Pacific Marine Mammal Center T-shirt. I had a full day ahead and, in my profession, comfort supersedes fashion. I saved the designer togs for the social occasions and, in Laguna, those occasions were plentiful.

I loved Laguna Beach. I loved my job. I loved my life. And as I pulled my silver vintage Mercedes convertible out of the driveway on such a gorgeous southern California morning, I was even more thankful for the beauty around me because it reminded me of how fragile life could be.

I knew nothing really about the man who'd been killed. Had it been planned? Or a crime of convenience where someone had taken the opportunity because of the chaos? Or had it simply been a tragic accident? As I knew from experience, life can change on a dime. There were more questions than answers, and it sounded like Laguna Beach Homicide and Detective Malone had their work cut out for them.

One thing Detective Malone had been clear about was he needed to talk with Verdi's brother. Well, I guess he'd been clear about two things. He'd also been crystal clear about the fact he was not going to return Grandma Tillie's brooch to me until the stabbing had been sorted out.

I didn't like it, but I guess it guaranteed a way to keep the pin safe from my cousin, Mel. I couldn't get it back, but Melinda also couldn't get to it as long as it was locked up in police evidence. For the first time, the brooch's location was absolutely Mel-proof.

I slipped on my sunglasses and lifted my face to the warmth of the early morning sun. I lived in The Village part of Laguna. There's also an area called the Top of the World, where the mansions cling to the steep hillsides like barnacles, and where they not only feel the touch of the sun first on the morning like this, but where they also have the most amazing views of the Pacific Ocean.

Then there are the gated communities: Emerald Bay, Ruby Point, Three Arch Bay, and the new one, Diamond Cove. Each of them has their own unique personality, but all are focused on keeping their residents safe and secure. The more Bohemian central downtown area has houses that are older, but often have a more artistic flare. The advantage of The Village is that you're close to all the great restaurants and shops. In my case, I could walk to work if I wanted. Days like this, I drove because I knew I had a full day of clients, and I usually see them in their homes. Much easier to sort out problems in the environment the pets are accustomed to.

The office parking lot was deserted when I arrived. It wasn't unusual for me to be the only one in on any given day. It depended on what my officemates had going on. As I entered the building, I could see the receptionist desk was empty. I stepped behind the desk to see if there was a note and quickly checked the calendar Verdi kept of which days she worked.

Shoot. This was a day she was off. She must be at her other job at the Koffee Klatch. I would have to try to catch her there between appointments.

I'd gathered the client files for my morning appointments when I heard a ding as someone came through the front entrance. Diana Knight poked her head into my office.

"I was on my way to the ARL for my volunteer stint and thought I'd stop by for a minute." She stepped through the doorway. In hot pink cropped jeans and a flattering coral and pink striped top, she looked years younger than her age. "Did I catch you at a bad time?"

"Not at all. I'm just getting ready to head out to see my first client of the day—a licking Labrador. The poor pup licks himself, his toys, the furniture, the floor, pretty much anything his tongue can reach."

"Aww, poor thing. I'm sure you'll sort it out."

"I hope so, for his sake."

Diana lowered her voice. "I wondered if you'd heard anything more about last night's incident." She looked around. "Verdi's not here?"

"No, this isn't one of her days in the office."

"Do you know if the police have talked to her?"

"I tried to call her. She wasn't next door at April Mae's." Verdi had been catsitting for my next-door neighbor who was out of town. "Verdi's such a nice kid, and her brother seemed to be the same. I hope it's a simple misunderstanding and he had a good reason for disappearing. Was Dino upset?"

"No, not at all."

"Did you know the guy who was stabbed?" I asked. "They didn't give his name on the news."

Diana knew everyone. At least everyone with enough cash to pay five thousand dollars a ticket for a Greyhound rescue event.

"Victor Lustig, I'm told was his name." As usual she had Mr. Wiggles, her Puggle, tucked into her handbag. "I'd heard he had rented the beach house out at Mission Point a few months ago. The owner's wife died last year, and the poor man went a little mad. Old coot is living most of the year in Palm Beach with some supermodel airhead about one-fifth his age. George Thomas, the old coot's attorney, manages the property for him, and he rented it to this guy, Victor. No one seems to know what exactly he did for a living."

As it turned out, Diana knew a lot more than most.

"Is the attorney the same George Thomas that's on the Greys Matter board?" I asked.

"That's him. George S. Thomas. I think the S stands for 'sloth.' The man hardly works. It's a good thing Greys Matter doesn't have much legal work."

"How did he get to be on the board?" I thought the positions were all volunteer.

"He inherited the position from his father, George P. Thomas. Nice man, the senior Thomas. And very sharp. The son, however, is no firecracker."

"Seems so odd." I placed the files I'd collected in my bag.

"What's odd?" Diana followed me into the outer office.

"That no one really knew this Victor Lustig."

"That is strange." Diana absently patted Mr. Wiggles's head. "I feel badly for Blanche. She does such an incredible job for the Greyhound rescue cause, and this event was to be the big fund-raiser."

"Hopefully this will be solved quickly."

"I bet it will. Let me know if there's anything I can do, Caro. You're an excellent judge of people, so I'm sure you're right about Verdi and her brother." She opened the door to leave. "I'd better get going."

"Okay, see you later."

The door closed behind her and I stood in the silence a few minutes. Diana was wrong. I was a lousy judge of people. That's how I'd been taken in by my ex-husband's charm, only to find he was an unfaithful, lying, unethical snake in the grass.

I'd thought in the time since the divorce, or "The Big Mess," as Mama likes to call it, I'd gotten better at recognizing lies and seeing through the fakes.

But what if I hadn't?

THE DAY WENT quickly and, after the Lab with the licking problem which was as I'd suspected really more of an anxiety issue (exercise and calm time prescribed), I'd moved on to a cat fight issue.

Not the type of cat fights I'd dealt with during my Texas beauty pageant days. This involved actual felines with prima donna attitudes. The family had an older cat and had introduced a young kitten with the idea it would encourage her to get some exercise. Instead, she'd become the grumpy dowager of the household. The old girl had become creative in showing her displeasure, and the new cat on the block was in hiding most of the time. We came up with some ideas to get the two together, and I had every confidence the two would adjust.

I'd scheduled a time to check back in a week with both the Licking Lab and the Ferocious Feline and their families.

I had no luck in catching Verdi at the Koffee Klatch. My appointments had all gone long, and I'd missed her. The afternoon was just as busy, and I didn't get a chance to try her cell again.

As I pulled into my drive, I noted there was no car next door, so Verdi must have already made her visit to Toby and Minou, her catsitting charges. I didn't think she was avoiding me, but she was probably feeling awkward about the situation.

Setting my groceries on the counter, I dropped my purse on the floor and kicked off my shoes. Thelma and Louise, my two cats, left their perch on the windowsill to come check out the groceries, and Dogbert trotted out to greet me.

My cell phone rang, and I glanced at the number but didn't recognize it. At least that meant it wasn't my mother. I was not in the mood for a "what are you doing," "who are you seeing,", "what are you eating," phone call from the Queen of I-Gave-Birth-to-You-So-You-Will- Listen-to-Me.

I answered the call. It was Blanche LeRue who wanted me to stop by the next day and check out her two Greyhounds who she felt had been traumatized by the craziness last night.

I could imagine they might be—I felt a little traumatized myself.

Chapter Four

I'VE NEVER BELIEVED much in women's intuition.

I think it comes from paying attention to what goes on around you. Sometimes you have to listen to what people are saying and sometimes you have to listen to what they're not saying. Mostly, you just have to shut up and listen.

As promised, I'd stopped by Blanche's house first thing. She lived in the house her grandparents had built in the 1920s. It was a Village Craftsman bungalow, sturdy and classic. Most days, Blanche was the same.

Today, she answered the door a bit out of breath, her expression startled like she wasn't expecting me. Had she forgotten she'd called me?

"Oh, where are my manners?" Blanche stepped to the side and motioned for me to enter. "Please come in."

Her home was comfortably furnished with Arts and Crafts-era antiques. An oak bookcase, a couple of Stickley chairs, a mission-style library table. Classy and solid.

I asked her to describe what her dogs had done to make her feel they were traumatized by their experience at the Greyhound event.

Blanche paced and circled as she talked, and the dogs followed her steps.

"I'm so worried about you two." She stopped for a moment, reached down and chucked each dog under the chin.

I'd only seen her at animal charity events, so I didn't know what her usual casual hang-around-home outfit was. But I guessed it wasn't a coffee-stained blouse and wrinkled slacks. Plus, I was pretty sure her usually sleek silver hair had not seen a brush today.

It could be that her Greyhounds, Blaze and Trixie, were agitated because of the incident at the fund-raiser as Blanche thought, or it could be the dogs had picked up on her agitation. Maybe I needed to calm the owner before I could deal with the dogs.

"Would it be possible to take them into your backyard?" I asked.

"Yes. I guess so." She indicated a path through to the back. "I don't want to get too far from the phone, though. I've left several messages for Dave at the Greys Matter foundation office and I'm expecting him to call me back."

"Perhaps you could take your cell phone." I pointed at the device lying on the table.

"Oh, my goodness. Of course. What am I thinking?" She grabbed the phone. "This isn't like me."

We walked through the kitchen and dining area toward the wide French doors. She had a beautiful house, but it wasn't difficult to tell that Greyhound dogs were her passion. There were pictures on every wall of different dogs. The hallway was lined with photos of Blanche with various celebrities who had helped with Greys Matter and the Greyhound adoption cause.

She hesitated, her hand on the doorknob. "I feel terrible that the fund-raiser went so badly." She sighed. "People brought their dogs to what we'd promised was a safe dog-friendly environment and then their beautiful babies were traumatized."

"And a man is dead," I pointed out.

"Oh." She stopped. "Of course. That sounded heartless, didn't it? I didn't mean it that way. The poor man. I don't want to minimize what happened, but I can't really do anything to help find out who killed him. The police will sort all that out."

"I'm sure they're working on it."

"But I do feel responsible for the dogs," she went on. "I'd like you to check with each of the owners for me, and if they need your services, I'll pay your fee for them. It's the least I can do."

"Let's start with Blaze and Trixie and we'll go from there." The two sighthounds were older and quite well-behaved.

The dogs slipped out as Blanche opened the door. They circled the small yard, nosed some dog toys by the small pool, and then settled in the shade.

Many people believe Greyhounds are busy animals because they're racers, but the truth is, they really are couch potatoes. When they chase, they run like the wind. The rest of the time they sleep, often up to eighteen hours a day. I could see why Blanche had thought there would be no problem bringing them to the charity event.

I glanced at the two dogs reclining at the side of the pool—the perfect relaxed socialites. At any moment I expected them to pull out their floppy hats and Ray-Bans.

Though Blanche had been worried about Blaze and Trixie, the truth was they seemed pretty calm. It was Blanche who remained traumatized.

Blanche lived alone. Maybe she just needed to talk.

"Have you heard anything from the police?"

Blanche tapped a fingernail on her phone. "Not a thing."

"How about *D'Orange Maison*?" I asked. "And where on earth did that rabbit come from?"

"No one seems to know." Blanche chewed her lip and ran a hand through her hair, making it stick up in several spots. The worry ate away at her usual polish.

"Do you have a list of the attendees?" I asked. "I'd be happy to follow up with the Greyhound owners."

"I don't have anything on paper. My handwriting is so awful." She lifted her hands. "I do everything on my little tablet computer. Let me find the spreadsheet and I'll email it to you."

She motioned me back in the house. I glanced at Blaze and Trixie who were still stretched out like sunbathers on the concrete.

As we stepped back inside, Blanche picked up a small tablet computer from the kitchen counter and asked for my email address. Then with a couple of swipes and taps, she was done.

"There you go," she said. "I get so frustrated with people my age who think they're too old to embrace technology. I love it. I keep my appointments, my contacts, all of my documents right here." She slid the tablet onto the counter. "Much better than a desk calendar, a handbag stuffed full of business cards, or a bunch of handwritten notes you can't read."

No doubt about it, Blanche LeRue disproved the idea you can't teach an old dog new tricks. I could see why Diana thought so highly of her. She was a woman to be reckoned with. She'd taken a hit; she might be flustered today, but she was a fighter. She'd be okay.

I said good-bye to Blanche and told her I'd make contact with each of the Greyhound owners and then would keep her apprised of who accepted her offer and of my follow-ups with them.

BACK AT THE office, I checked my email and downloaded the list of Greyhound owners Blanche had sent through cyberspace. There weren't fifty, thank God. Some of them weren't local, some owners had multiple dogs. Still, in any event, it was a lot of appointments.

Blanche had asked that I bill her instead of the Greyhound rescue and I had agreed, full well knowing I'd do the follow-ups gratis.

Every board member except for Sam and Diana had Greyhounds. Sam had gotten conned into being a Greys Matter board member by Diana and by his grandmother. It wasn't that Sam wasn't a dog person, but a Greyhound wouldn't have been a good choice for him. Couch potato and Sam didn't belong in the same sentence. He needed a dog as active as he was.

Sam was a catch in his own right, but I'd resisted his invitations at first. What I'd found I couldn't hold out against was that the man also owned the dog of my dreams, a handsome Border Collie named Mac. Some women picked their dates based on their portfolio. I picked my dates based on their pets.

Sam's grandmother had two of the small Italian Greyhounds. Ari and Angel were sweet, well-behaved dogs, and she doted on them. They'd been in attendance at the Fifty Shades event.

Alana and Dave Benda also had the two Italian Greyhounds we'd talked about when Alana had been sizing up my fashion sense. I could probably try to catch Dave at the office to ask about them, but he was in and out so much, I decided to try Alana instead. I called but got voicemail so left her a message. I made a note.

Scheduling all these appointments would be a daunting task on top of my normal client load. And I still needed to talk to Verdi about Eugene.

Thinking I could mark two things off my list at once, I called Verdi's cell. I would enlist her help in organizing the appointments, and it would give us a chance to talk. Again, voicemail. Did no one answer their phones anymore?

Next on my list was to call Detective Malone and get my brooch back. I had no hope for anything but voicemail this time.

Before I could make the call to Malone, my cell phone rang.

I glanced at the number. This time is was my mother. If I didn't bite the bullet and take her call, she'd just keep trying. The woman was Texas tough and Montgomery stubborn. There was a good chance if I avoided her calls for too long, she'd just show up on my doorstep.

That would not be good.

I sighed the sigh of guilt-ridden daughters everywhere and hit the answer button.

Okay, deep breath. I was a grown woman. I could do this.

"Good morning, Mama."

"Carolina Lamont, why are you determined to make me look stupid in front of my own family?"

There was to be no salutation. We were apparently going from zero to a full heaping of blame without even a hello. And I didn't even know what I'd done.

I counted to ten and then asked, "How, pray tell, have I done that from this distance?"

Big old sigh on her end and then silence. I could tell she was smoothing her eyebrow with her index finger, like she always did when she was particularly irritated with me.

I broke first. "I haven't even talked to any of the family."

"Maybe not." She had shifted the phone by now so she could admire her manicure. I didn't need video-conferencing to get the picture. "I had lunch with my sister, Barbara, and I had to hear the news from her." She paused, either to catch her breath or for effect. Perhaps both.

"What news?" The only thing I could think was that someone had told Mama I was once again involved in a murder investigation.

"I have to hear from my sister that my own daughter is about to marry a billionaire olive tycoon."

"What?" I screeched.

"There is no reason to yell at me, young lady." Mama Kat said sharply in the same tone she'd used when I was eighteen and came home late. "I am not the one keeping secrets."

I am going to kill Mel.

She *knew* what would happen if she planted even the slightest hint that I was serious about Sam Gallanos. With the two sisters, our mothers, together, the hint would spark the idea we were serious. And that spark would become a wildfire, and now Mama had us picking out china patterns.

Deep breath.

"Mama, I am not about to marry anyone."

"But Melinda told Barbara—"

"She was just teasin'." I wanted to say more, but it wasn't Mama's fault she'd been played. "You know Mel."

"You're sure you're not keeping things from me?"

I was not going to answer that question directly.

Let's see, there was this guy who died at my feet a couple of nights ago.

And as for Sam, I couldn't really explain what I didn't know myself. He'd like us to be more. I still had a lot of baggage.

"Mama, hon, if there comes a time when I'm fixing to be engaged, I promise, I will let you know."

"You really aren't?"

"I absolutely am not."

She wasn't happy but dropped the topic. But we weren't done. She went on to a series of family updates and Dallas society gossip. I did my daughterly duty and listened. Sort of.

By the time we hung up, I was sure of a couple of things.

First, I'd think twice before I took a call on the fly from my mother. Second, I didn't know how, but I would find a way to get even with my cousin.

Game on, Melinda.

Chapter Five

I'VE FOUND THE best way to deal with a daunting task is to tackle it.

I couldn't deal with Mel and her mischief right away. I'd had no luck with Malone and the brooch, but I had finally reached Verdi. She'd agreed to help me over lunch the next day with organizing the list of Greyhound owners whom I needed to contact. I truly needed the help, and I also thought it might give us a chance to talk.

So, the following day, after a couple of morning appointments, I picked up two salads and headed to the office.

Verdi looked up as I came through the doorway. You could tell she, like Blanche, wasn't herself. Her ready smile was absent, her face was pale, her eyes held the traces of a sleepless night, and even her burgundy hair drooped.

"Everyone out?" I asked.

"They are." She pushed aside the mail she'd been sorting. "Kay is showing a house. I haven't heard from Dave. Suzanne isn't scheduled in until three o'clock for her first appointment."

A real estate broker, an accountant, a psychic, and a pet therapist. Only in Laguna, huh? I often said, our office lineup sounds like the beginning to a bad joke. Still, it worked for us. And Verdi had been a great addition for us. Our office needs were few, but we appreciated having someone as well-organized as Verdi to sort the mail, pay the bills, and keep track of the details for us.

"I brought us some lunch. Come on in and eat with me." I motioned her to follow as I carried the files I'd used that morning and the takeout bag. Verdi had just brewed some green tea, and she carried a couple of glasses into my office.

We made quick work of the list Blanche had emailed to me. Verdi added a column for location and quickly re-sorted into groups by location.

"I'll call each set of owners and use your calendar to schedule appointments," she said. "If they're not interested, I'll note that in the comments."

"Thanks, hon. I sure appreciate the help." I smiled at her. "Now let's eat."

I set out the salads, and we settled into the comfy chairs. We were both silent for a few moments.

"I'm sure the police talked to you." I kept my voice neutral.

"Yeah." She picked at the spinach and avocado on her salad. "Detective Malone came to my apartment."

"The night of the fund-raiser?" I asked.

Verdi nodded. Even with her Goth-girl look, the kid was as cute as a speckled pup, but right now, she was one dejected puppy. "I don't know where Eugene is. I don't know why he took off. But I know he didn't do it." Her voice quivered on the last word.

"Have you heard from him?" I had to ask.

She shook her head. "I know the detective didn't believe me, but I haven't."

"Your parents named you Verdi, but your twin brother is named Eugene?" It had been bothering me for a while, and I just had to ask. Not that all twins had to have similar names, but the two monikers seemed very dissimilar.

She popped a whole wheat crouton in mouth and chewed.

"No, my given name is Eugenia." She laid the salad box aside and folded her legs under her. "I had it legally changed to Verdi when I was old enough. My mom and dad didn't understand, but Eugenia just doesn't fit who I am. It was more about how they saw me. I had to be myself."

"I see." I really did. No one knew better than I about breaking away from a parent's expectations. Mama had been fit to be tied when I'd told her no more beauty pageants.

"Our parents weren't bad, but they were very restrictive. Eugene rebelled by getting into trouble. I rebelled in other ways." She touched her maroon locks with a slight smile. "Our family's kind of difficult to explain."

I could understand about difficult-to-explain families.

Heck, I had a cousin in town I wasn't speaking to, and a mother out of town who I fervently wished was not speaking to me.

"Do your folks live here in Orange County?"

"No, they're not even in California anymore. They moved north to Oregon. I have a phone number for them, but I'm not going to call and tell them Eugene is in trouble."

"I know, sugar." I wanted to hug the girl, she looked so darned fragile. "I'm afraid, though, that the police will contact them trying to find Eugene."

She looked up, startled. Apparently, that idea hadn't occurred to her.

"That would be worse, wouldn't it, hon?"

She gulped and nodded.

"Let's talk about where Eugene might have gone. Do you know his friends? Are they here in town? Would he have left the area?"

"I don't know, Caro. He had a bunch of geeky friends in high school, but he doesn't keep in touch with any of them as far as I know. Then Eugene went to college, which is where he met the hacker guy who got him in so much trouble. He did some bad stuff, got caught, and ended up in prison."

I let the silence sit for a while.

All at once, she leaned forward and dropped her feet to the floor. "I just had a thought. At one point he worked for a video game shop in Huntington Beach. The owner, Kyle, was a good friend of his."

"Do you have a phone number for this guy?"

"No, but it wouldn't be too hard to get." She took a sip of her green tea. "I don't know the name of the place, but I know where the shop is."

"Great. I could go in there and pretend to, I don't know, need something. And try to find out if this guy has been in touch with your brother."

Verdi choked on her tea.

"No, you couldn't." Her gaze pointedly traveled the length of my person. From my Alexander McQueen tee, to my designer jeans, to my new Dolce and Gabbana wedge sandals.

"I'll wear a disguise." I could change my look. I knew from walking by the game shop in downtown Laguna, I'd need to tone things down a bit.

"This I gotta see." Verdi smiled for the first time since we'd started talking. "It's more than the clothes, Caro. I'm not sure you could lose that beauty pageant posture if your life depended on it."

True, the posture had been bred through hours of practice—like a show horse. After years of beauty pageant training, it'd become second nature, but I was pretty sure I could lose it if my life depended on it. Of course, I hoped it didn't.

"I might surprise you." I smiled back.

"We'll see what we can do." She tipped her head to one side. "I think I can come up with a disguise that will make you blend in with the video game crowd. I don't think any of the people from the shop will even remember me."

"Wonderful. We have a plan." I smiled at her.

"Thanks for doing this, Caro." Verdi was suddenly serious. "I appreciate your help, and I'll owe you."

Yes, she would. Oh, heck, yes she would.

Chapter Six

IT TURNED OUT Verdi's idea of a disguise was much different than mine. Angelina Jolie had nothing on me. I had been transformed into Lara Croft, Tomb Raider. Verdi's borrowed black wig covered my red hair, but I still felt conspicuous. The motorcycle boots Verdi had provided meant at least I didn't have the additional lift of heels, but there was an uncomfortably large gap between the boots and the short-shorts part of the outfit. I'd worn skimpier outfits for swimsuit competitions back in my beauty pageant days, but it seemed different.

Maybe because then everyone else was in a swimsuit.

This ensemble covered more of me, but the midriff-baring T-shirt had a few subtle differences. For instance, it was crisscrossed with straps holding fake weapons. Fake, but pretty dang realistic-looking. More fake weapons were strapped to my thighs.

How, in heaven's name, was I supposed to sit?

Verdi, on the other hand, was some Zelda person. All elf-like and completely covered.

"I think we should trade," I told her.

"We can't, Caro." She folded our street clothes and laid them aside. "This wouldn't fit you. You're too tall. You make a great Lara."

"Okay," I said, resigned to my danger-chick look. "Let's get this over with."

"All the gamers won't look like this," she explained. "Some will look like they never leave their mother's basement, and others will look like regular business execs or retail clerks. This just makes us not look like us."

That was a Texas-sized understatement.

Verdi added a little more eyeliner to my look, although I didn't see how there was room for more. "This is the easiest way to disguise you and make you look like you belong. You'll—you know—blend in."

"This makes me blend in?" I pointed at my exposed tummy and the skintight leather short-shorts.

I was afraid Verdi would have to drive us and I'd have to lie down in the backseat to keep from splitting my britches.

The video game store was called End Game and was in a strip mall just across the imaginary line into Huntington Beach. We found a parking spot near the entrance.

I was glad because I didn't want to have to walk too far in my skimpy "blend-in" full-body action figure garb. The motorcycle boots were pretty darned comfortable, and I wondered about the possibility of working them into a fashion look. I'd seen my cousin, Melinda, wear them before and now I understood why.

As we stepped into the store, the guy behind the counter looked up and grunted, "Huh." The two of us in our outfits fazed him not at all.

Verdi moved through the aisles, and I followed. We pretended to look at the vintage comics on the back wall. There was a girl with pure-white spiky hair who sorted stock while carrying on a conversation with a guy who actually did look like a business executive. Granted, a very young biz guy with tattoos and multiple piercings, but still.

"Hey," Verdi greeted them as she stepped between them.

"Huh." I tipped my head, thinking it was a good mimic of the guy up front. I followed Verdi, reminding myself, *no beauty pageant posture.*

She turned and looked at the two. "Either of you know Kyle Wahler?"

They both paused what they were doing. The girl turned to look at us.

"Why?" She stretched out one leg and adjusted her blue sparkly snowflake-covered hoodie.

The guy looked me over head to toe. "Epic," he pronounced.

"He gonna be in?" Verdi answered the girl's question with a question.

"Not today." The girl went back to stacking movies. "He's off."

"'Kay." Verdi had perfected feigned disinterest.

I stood by, leaning my leather-clad hip against a display.

"Is there a message?" The guy seemed slightly more helpful, but still overly interested in my um . . . weapons.

"I owe him money," I said.

Verdi turned to look at me. We should have talked more about our strategy before we embarked on this little adventure. Time was of the essence in finding her brother.

"You can come back tomorrow," the girl said.

"We're just in town for the day." We needed to push.

"Does he live nearby?" It was worth a try. "We can drop the money off at his house."

"Yeah, he's got a house in Oak View."

"Got an address?"

"Yeah, but I don't know if he'll be there or not." He picked up a scrap of paper and plucked little Miss Jack Frost's pen from her hand.

He wrote on both sides of the paper and handed us the note.

"Thanks." We'd done it!

I was afraid to look at Verdi for fear my expression would change.

We walked back to Verdi's car, trying not to move too quickly in case the crew at End Game watched. It would be awful to come this close and have Kyle spooked.

Once we were in the car, though, all bets were off.

"Score!" Verdi squealed.

"Epic score!" I returned.

Okay, maybe I'd gotten into my role a little too much.

I looked at the note. Biz guy had written Kyle's address on one side and his name and phone on the other side. I couldn't decide if I was flattered or creeped out by being hit on by a younger man.

I read the address to Verdi.

"Do you know the area?" I assumed we were going directly to Kyle's.

"Oh, yeah." She'd already started the car. "I can find it."

IT WAS DUSK by the time we pulled onto Kyle's street. Large palms and eucalyptus trees lined the boulevard, making it seem darker than it was.

We parked a block away and sat for a few moments watching the house. There were no lights on, but there was a flicker behind the curtains, like someone was watching television or, given what we knew about Kyle, maybe playing a video game.

"Shall we?" I glanced at Verdi. She fidgeted with her collar, pulled it up, patted it down. She looked as nervous as I felt.

"Sugar, if you want, we can call Detective Malone and let him handle this."

She shook her head. "I just want to see if I can find Eugene and talk to him. Convince him to talk to the police. It will look better if he goes to them."

"Okay then." I knew calling Malone was the better plan, but

shoot, if it were my brother, I'd feel the same way. "Ready?"

Verdi nodded and opened her door.

We approached the front of the house, a boxy beige stucco surrounded by a wrought-iron fence, and knocked.

No one came to the door.

After a few minutes, we tried again. We could still see the flicker of light.

Verdi shrugged. "Maybe if he's playing a video game, he's got headphones on and can't hear us knock."

"Let's go around to the back. Maybe we can see in."

We made our way around the house opening the iron gate. Kyle could use a good landscaping service. It looked like there'd been an attempt at cleanup at one point, but an unsuccessful one.

There was a patio in back with a nice grill and a few lawn chairs gathered around it. Through the back windows, we could see the light more clearly. It did look like there could be someone in the house.

"Should we knock?" Verdi asked.

"Why not?" At this point, while I wanted to help Verdi, my motives had become a little more selfish. Sure, I wanted to find out if Kyle knew where Eugene was. But mostly, I wanted to get home and get out of the Tomb Raider outfit.

I lifted my hand and pounded on the back door. "Hello," I called. "Is anyone home?

No response.

I shrugged and tried the door, turning the knob to see if the house was locked. There was a slight pause and then an awful shrieking filled the air. You know the sound car alarms make? Like that, only ten times louder.

Verdi and I looked at each other in shock, turned, and ran.

We rounded the corner of the house and skidded to a halt.

"Stop right there."

Three official-looking tough guys with guns drawn blocked our escape.

"Keep your hands where we can see them," the taller one in the middle ordered.

I carefully raised my black leather-gloved hands in the air, taking no chances that the guys with real guns might think I was going for my plastic weapons.

Chapter Seven

THE MEN MARCHED us to the front of the house, cuffed us, and parked us on the steps.

Uncomfortable, I pulled the hem of my shorts down as much as I could, considering the handcuffs, and adjusted my plastic guns so I wasn't in danger of poking Verdi and her sword.

The taller gray-haired guy who seemed to be in charge stood over us. "Would you like to explain yourselves?"

I looked at Verdi in her green elf outfit and then down at my don't-mess-with-this-chick black leather Tomb Raider garb. I wasn't sure there was a good explanation for the way we were dressed, but I imagined the man meant more than our attire.

"We're looking for her brother." I shifted on the uncomfortable concrete.

"Does he live here?" His face was granite.

"No," Verdi answered.

"Then why were you breaking into this house?" Mr. Serious looked from Verdi to me and back again.

"We weren't breaking in," I answered. "I tried the door because it looked like a television was on, and we thought maybe someone really was home and hadn't heard us knock."

"Is your brother missing?" He nailed Verdi with a don't-lie-to-me look.

"Not exactly." Verdi looked away.

"Either he is or he isn't." The man reached inside his jacket and put away his weapon. "Do you have identification?"

"I do, but it's in the car." Verdi pointed to her little green Fiat parked up the street.

He shifted his intense gaze to me. "And you?"

There hadn't really been any room in the skimpy shorts, and I wasn't driving so I'd left my bag back at the house. "No, I'm sorry, not with me."

He turned to look at one of the other men. "Take this one to get her ID." Then he turned back to me. "Your name?"

"Carolina Lamont." I answered. "And you are?" Up to this point, he hadn't said.

"John Milner, FBI."

Holy Eliot Ness!

We were in deeper doo-doo than I'd thought. What was the FBI doing at Kyle's house? I'd assumed these guys were undercover cops already in the neighborhood for some reason and when they'd heard the alarm thought we were burglars. Okay, there was a rather large hole in my theory that involved the fact that, as far as I knew, burglars usually didn't wear video game character costumes. But still, FBI?

The other FBI agent came back with Verdi and handed her driver's license to Agent Milner.

"Run this." Milner handed the license back. "And also check the name Carolina Lamont."

"What's he checking for?" Verdi asked.

"Outstanding warrants, among other things," Agent Milner answered. "Make yourselves comfortable, ladies." He walked a short distance away, but not so far away he couldn't hear us talk.

Verdi and I settled in to wait. I shifted on the step and straightened my legs. I lifted one combat-booted foot and crossed my ankles. I felt ridiculous. Here I was, a grown woman, dressed up as a video game character. Parked on a front step and handcuffed. Not one of my finer moments.

The only thing that could have completed my humiliation was if someone I knew drove by.

It seemed like hours before the agent who'd been instructed to run our names came back. He and Milner stepped a little farther away and turned their backs to us. I imagined to discuss our fate.

Agent Milner came back to the front step and handed Verdi's license to her. "Young lady, it seems your brother is a person of interest in a murder investigation." His voice was neutral but still said he was serious as a heart attack. "I assume you're aware of that fact?"

Verdi nodded.

"And you." Mr. Serious shifted his attention to me. "Seems you've been involved a couple of times with local law enforcement."

"Not in a bad way, though." I couldn't be held accountable for a dead client or next-door neighbor who'd been shot. And I'd helped the police, not been in trouble with them. I was sure there would be nothing as far as an official record about my involvement. What in the

Sam Hill kind of database were they searching?

Agent Milner sighed. "Okay, stand up."

We stood, and he uncuffed Verdi and me.

I rubbed my wrists. The cuffs hadn't really hurt, but had kind of chafed the skin. "Are we free to go then?"

You know the thought I'd had earlier?

The one about the only thing that could make the situation more embarrassing? Yeah, well, just as I thought we were free to get out of Dodge, a silver Camaro pulled up beside the curb and Detective Judd Malone got out.

He approached the group and introduced himself to the agents. Then he turned and got a good look at Verdi and me.

A bark of a laugh slipped out before he could catch himself.

"Ms. Lamont, Ms. Perry." He got the words out, but failed in his attempt to get his face back to an official cop-like expression. He tried to speak again, but couldn't contain himself. He doubled over, his shoulders shaking. Although Agent Milner had found no humor in the situation at all, it seemed Detective Malone found it hilarious. While I'd wondered at times if the man had a sense of humor, this was not the way I wanted to find out that he did.

"These are the women we talked to you about," Agent Serious intoned, his eyes fixed on us like a Great Dane on guard duty. No distractions for him. I doubted the man even knew how to smile. "We can release them into your custody if you'll vouch for them."

"What?" My head jerked up. "We don't want to be released to him."

After a short conversation with the FBI fellows, Malone walked us to Verdi's car. He'd composed himself, but every once in a while a grin twitched at his lips and an inadvertent chuckle broke loose.

Detective Malone stood on the curb, hands stuffed in the pockets of his jeans, while Verdi and I silently got into the Fiat. He leaned down and looked at us before closing the passenger side door. "You drive carefully," he cautioned Verdi. "I'd hate to see you two hotshots get stopped for speeding."

Verdi started the car, and we drove off. As we made the turn at the corner, I could still see Malone shaking his head and grinning.

As for Zelda and I, we headed back to Laguna Beach to retrieve our regular clothes and, I hoped and prayed, our sanity.

IT PROBABLY SOUNDS anticlimactic after the adventures of the day, but I needed a little less drama in my life. All I wanted was an escape, so I spent the rest of the evening reading in bed. Thelma and Louise, my trusty felines, and Dogbert, my wonderful mutt, cuddled against me.

Finally, I gave up trying to concentrate and turned off the light, but sleep didn't come easily.

My mind kept looking for answers. Who was Victor Lustig, and why had he been killed? What was the FBI was doing watching Eugene's friend's house? And, when I wasn't trying to sort those things out, I kept torturing myself with the picture of Detective Malone's mirth as we'd driven away.

Chapter Eight

THE OFFICE WAS quiet when I arrived the next morning.

Verdi had left me a note. The day's appointments were filled. She had contacted each of the people on the Greyhound aftermath list, and, surprisingly, most of them wanted to be seen. I wasn't sure if they really had dog issues or if they wanted to know if I knew any details about the murder. The media had stopped reporting on the whole debacle, I supposed because there hadn't been any sort of break in the murder case. They'd moved on to other news: gang fights, stock market reports, celebrity rehab details. Life went on.

I picked up the files I needed for the morning. In addition to the Greyhound parents on the schedule, I had a house call nearby in the Village, with Brandi, a new client. And then a short visit in the lavish Ruby Point gated community with Davis Pinter and Huntley, his Cavalier King Charles Spaniel. It would be a full morning.

The appointment with Brandi and her dogs took very little time. Brandi was a well-heeled Laguna resident who lived in the southern part of town where she was able to have a big yard. She answered the door and invited me in, moving easily in her wheelchair.

Brandi had two dogs, both rescues: Katy, an eleven-year-old blue heeler whom she'd had since the dog was four months old, and Bailey, a two-year-old brindle-colored Border Collie.

As you know, I'm a big sucker for a Border Collie. They're really smart dogs and very teachable, often even learning words. The breed is ranked number one in several texts that rank the intelligence, of dogs and they're typically extremely energetic and acrobatic.

I'd had one growing up and would have ten today if I had the room. Bailey was a little spitfire and, as Brandi explained, was an all-star player in the ball-fielding department.

Katy, the other dog, was a little more aloof and was not as quick to get to know me. She was all business and clearly wondered why I was there. If there were a canine version of Neil Simon's *Odd Couple*, Katy would be Felix Unger. Though we commonly refer to them as blue-heelers or red-heelers, the breed is actually the Australian Cattle Dog. Though I worried about two in-charge herding types in one household, it was clear it worked well for Brandi and her family.

I, much like Katy, wondered why I was there.

Brandi, as it turned out, wanted to talk to me about Miss Katy and her reaction to storms. We don't get a lot of rainstorms in southern California, but when they occurred, it seemed to create a lot of anxiety for Katy. It wasn't the noise because SoCal storms aren't the big loud gullywashers like we get at home. There's nothing like the sudden fury and pounding rain of a Texas thunderstorm.

I asked Brandi to describe the dog's behavior. After hearing a few of her accounts of Katy's pacing and running from room to room, and their unsuccessful attempts to calm her, I thought I had Katy's problem pegged.

It wasn't so much the dog was feeling fear. She was simply protective of her herd, which was Brandi and the rest of her family. I recommended letting her check on everyone.

"Don't try to settle her down." I patted Katy's head as I talked, but Bailey soon nosed in as well, sliding her head under my hand. "Let her go room to room and do her thing. She'll settle herself once she's verified everyone is accounted for."

I tossed a ball and Bailey bounded after it, ready to play.

I was so glad Brandi had called. I'd had a great time with her and her two dogs.

Leaving my card with Brandi, I asked her to keep in touch and to let me know how Katy did with the new approach to her anxious behavior. Also, I'd had a thought: Dogbert would love her two dogs. We might just make plans to stop by for a play date.

Next, I headed to Ruby Point where Davis Pinter, the retired newspaper tycoon, was on the docket. We'd worked together before and Huntley had very few problems. However, they were going to be traveling and Davis had some questions. He was also a great dog owner and took daily walks with Huntley. Cavaliers are super companion dogs and perfect for a retiree like Davis.

The prize-winning newsman routinely called me for consultations. Partly, I believed, because he was bored. The excitement of the newsroom was a thing of the past, and Davis hadn't really taken to the slower pace of retirement.

Both clients, human and dog, were in the backyard when I arrived. Davis had set out a pitcher of lemonade on the patio table and offered me a glass. Never one to refuse a refreshment, I accepted.

"Have a seat, Caro." He pulled out a chair and poured drinks for us both.

Davis's home was one of the nicer homes in Ruby Point, but the patio was my favorite part. A flagstone path led from the house to a small oasis of green hedges and colorful flowerbeds. Like most of the homes in the gated community, he had a swimming pool in the back, but his was made from natural rocks and the water babbled across them, sounding like a mountain stream if you sat quietly.

"Thanks, Davis." I slid into the comfortable seat in the shade and slipped my sunglasses off. "How are you doing? I haven't seen you since the Greyhound event. You look good."

Older but far from elderly, Davis had salt-and-pepper hair that gave him a distinguished look, and the man was always sharply dressed. Less formal than the last time I'd seen him, but he wore still-creased tan chinos and a boldly-striped shirt that looked freshly pressed.

"I'm doing fine. That was quite the deal. I was clear across the room, so they questioned me and sent me on my way rather quickly." He took a sip of his lemonade and smiled down at Huntley who had joined us. "What about you, Caro? You were right near the guy, weren't you?"

"I was." I explained about thinking the man had been having a panic attack, only to find he'd been stabbed.

"Good grief." He leaned forward to scratch Huntley's head. "That had to be unsettling."

"It was a little surreal," I admitted.

"What's the story?" Davis's brow furrowed. "Have you heard anything on the case?"

"Not a thing. Eugene Perry, one of the catering workers and the twin brother of Verdi, our receptionist at the office, is a 'person of interest,' at least according to Detective Malone."

"Why is that?"

Though Davis was retired from the newsroom, I don't think the curiosity that made him good at digging for a story had gone into retirement.

"Mainly because he disappeared that night and hasn't been heard from since."

"Hmm." He wrinkled his forehead. "Doesn't mean he's guilty, but it doesn't look good, does it? What does his sister say?"

"She says he had some trouble when he was younger. Computer

hacking. Went to jail, but he's cleaned up his act. She hasn't heard from him or been able to locate him."

I didn't mention our trip to the computer store.

Or run-in with the FBI.

Or the costumes.

"Who was the guy that was stabbed?"

"That's the odd thing. New in town. No one seems to have known him. At least not very well or for very long. He had attended social gatherings around town."

"The news didn't give his name. Said they were looking for relatives."

"It was Victor Lustig," I supplied.

"What?" Davis sat up straight. "Did you say *Victor Lustig*?"

"I'm sure that's what Diana told me. Why? Do you know the name?"

"I sure do." Davis chuckled. "And you should, too. That's the name of a legendary con man. He's the guy that sold the Eiffel Tower. Twice, in fact."

"No kidding?" No wonder the name had seemed slightly familiar to me. I'd been trying to remember, thinking it was someone I knew.

"I'd say something's not quite what it seems with our murder victim."

"I'd say you're right."

"Makes me sorry I'm leaving town." Davis lifted the pitcher. "Would you like some more?"

"No, thank you." I'd enjoyed the lemonade and the conversation but needed to get back to the reason I was there. "Let's discuss your concerns about traveling with Huntley. Cavaliers travel very well. What, specifically, are you worried about?"

It turned out it wasn't the travel part that concerned Davis. He was going to stay with his daughter in Connecticut for a couple of weeks, and she had two tropical birds. Davis hadn't stayed at her house since she'd had the birds, and he knew Cavaliers have a strong sporting instinct, so he was mostly worried about the mix of Huntley and the birds.

While the bird flushing and hunting instinct is very strong in the breed, I explained, some Cavaliers do just fine in a home with birds. However, others do not. My suggestion was to discuss the concern with his daughter and perhaps keep the birds and dog separated or contained. If the birds were free, Huntley should be on his leash. If he was off leash, the birds should be caged. If the daughter was as responsible a pet owner as I knew Davis to be, I was sure they'd do fine.

I finished my drink, gave Huntley a snuggle, and wished Davis a good visit with his daughter. I could hardly wait to call Malone and ask if he'd realized the name of the stabbing victim had been fake. I was sure he had, and, of course, they would have run Victor's fingerprints, so maybe they already knew who he really was.

I called Malone from my car, but got his voicemail, so I left a message for him to call me. Again.

My next home visit was in Dana Point, so I turned the car south and enjoyed the beautiful drive along the Pacific Coast with the convertible top down. As I drove, I mulled the idea of why a man would choose a legendary con man's moniker as his name. Where had that idea come from? Why did he need a fake identity? And why had someone wanted him dead?

This call was one of the Greyhound owners Blanche had asked me to check on. Verdi had set up the appointment and supplied the address. I found the house without trouble and parked in the driveway.

It was a stunning contemporary home, modest compared to the Ruby Point mansions, but with a panoramic view of the Pacific and of Catalina Island. Marjory Whedon answered the door and welcomed me. She was tall and willowy, and her white linen pants and flowing turquoise top blended with the Zen feel of the house. The inside continued the modern lines.

Water flowed from a fountain in the foyer and created a feeling of serenity. I almost felt like I should offer to take off my shoes. The entryway opened into a living room which was nearly all glass on one side. I didn't blame them—I'd want a glass house too, if I had that view.

There were two white leather couches facing each other, and at one end were two Greyhounds sound asleep cuddled against each other.

"This must be Havasu and Jett." I glanced down at my file. "Havasu is the blue, and Jett is the black. Is that right?"

"That's right," Marjory answered. "Please, have a seat."

I perched on the edge of the white sofa near the two dogs. "Have you noticed any behavior changes since the night of the fund-raiser or have there been any problems?"

"No, no changes." She settled on the other coach, leaned back and crossed her legs. "To tell you the truth, this is how they usually are. I have to encourage them to go outside for a walk or they'd just stay put right here."

"They're striking dogs." I reached out and touched the black one who was closest to me. The dog raised its head, looked at me, and then settled back in. "Have you had them long?"

"Only a few months." Marjory shifted a little. "Raymond, my husband, met Alice Tiburon at some business function. She introduced him to Blanche at Greys Matter, and, once we heard about the situation with Greyhounds who no longer race, we simply had to help."

She got up, knelt by the dogs, and laid her cheek against them. "I have to say, Ms. Lamont, until that night, I'd had my doubts these two were truly retired racers. I'd never seen them run that fast."

"Call me Caro." I could tell she was truly attached to the dogs. "It was a mess, wasn't it?"

"Yes, it was. That poor man." She shivered slightly, as if shaking off the thought.

"Did you know him?" I couldn't help but ask.

"No, I didn't." She shook her head. "We talked about it coming home that night, and Raymond thought he might have seen him a couple of weeks ago at the Greys Matter office."

"Really?" That didn't match up for a couple of reasons, one of which was that Blanche claimed she didn't know Victor.

"Well, that's what he said, but he wasn't sure." She got up from her spot on the floor. "He'd stopped in to get copies of some additional paperwork we needed on Jett and Havasu for our vet, and he was in a hurry."

"And about Jett and Havasu," I said, changing the subject. "Do you have any concerns?"

"Not really," Marjory sat on the couch beside me. "Raymond and I discussed it when your assistant called. While we haven't seen any problems, we thought it was a good idea to find out what types of things we should be watching for."

"Mainly changes in their normal behavior, any loss of appetite, or nervous habits such as obsessive pacing," I explained. "Basically, any signs of anxiety or anything that doesn't feel right to you."

"So far, we've not seen anything like that."

"That's good." I gathered my things and stood. "It's clear your two are well taken care of and loved."

Marjory beamed. "They bring a lot of love to our home."

"If you do see any changes, just call my office." I handed her my card. "I'd be happy to come back."

"Thank you, Caro." She walked me to the door. "I feel so relieved."

I grabbed a quick lunch while I was in Dana Point, and then took care of my afternoon appointments before heading home for the day. I was so late that I didn't even go by the office to drop off my files and finish my notes.

Sometime tomorrow I'd stop by the Greys Matter office and talk with Blanche. I needed to let her know the status of the list of clients anyway, and perhaps I could work in a question about whether Victor, or whatever his name really was, had been at the rescue's office. And why she'd lied.

Chapter Nine

I WAS LATE FOR my very first self-defense class.

It had been such a busy day, I'd forgotten about it, so I'd had to rush to get there. The class was called "Be Safe" and Sam had gifted both Diana and me with the six-week course for Valentine's Day. You have to love a guy with a sense of humor.

As I walked into the room and looked around at all the trendy workout wear, I wished I'd paid a bit more attention to my attire. I'd run home, slipped on my yoga clothes, and headed to the fitness studio where the class was being held.

Diana was already there. She sported an orange Splits59 workout set. All the other women were similarly dressed in designer fitness togs. On the other hand, I'd thrown on old black yoga pants and a gray Nike tank top. Oh, well. I was there to learn, not to look fashionable, right?

Even as I had the thought, I could hear my mama's voice in my head saying, "Young lady, there is no reason you can't do both."

Our instructor was Matt Bjarni. A big, red-headed beefcake. If you ever needed to cast a bodybuilder type in a movie, you'd pick him.

Matt took us through an overview of what we would cover in the six weeks of sessions while two female assistants passed out brochures. The philosophy of the "Be Safe" program was to teach people to deal with real-world situations. I was happy to see avoidance and de-escalation of a situation were covered topics. It was all well and good to know some defensive moves, but the best case would be to never have to use them.

There were a variety of ages in the class. One mature lady in the front appeared to have come in her pajamas. Leopard print no less. Accessorized with a single strand of pearls.

At the moment, it sounded as if she were instructing Matt on proper classroom etiquette. Bless his heart, he just politely nodded.

The assistants had completed their work and joined him at the front of the room.

Matt faced the group. "Okay, let's get started. The most important thing to remember about keeping yourself safe is not the defensive moves I'm going to show you. The most important thing is to try to stay out of dangerous situations."

Diana and I looked at each other.

"Do you think Sam paid him to say that?" Diana muttered under her breath.

"Maybe," I whispered back. "Sure sounds like Sam, doesn't it?"

"If you do find yourself in a dangerous situation, your most valuable weapon is your brain." Matt walked back and forth as he talked. "Use your wits. Don't panic. Try to defuse before you defend."

The lady in the pajamas had her hand in the air.

Matt either didn't see it or was ignoring her.

Undeterred, she eagerly waved it back and forth.

Matt sighed a sigh we could hear even in the back of the room. He stopped in front of her. "Yes, ma'am. You have a question?"

"Name's Betty. And you're darn tootin' I do, Mike."

"It's Matt." He smiled. It was hard not to smile at the picture she presented in her leopard-print nightwear.

"I work retail," Pajama Betty said. "What if I've got a shoplifter? I don't have time for chitchat. I'm gonna have to move quick." She made what appeared to be some karate type slices with her hands.

"We'll get to those kinds of situations later." Matt dodged the deadly weapons, aka Betty's silk pajama-clad arms. "For now, let's talk about how to avoid situations where you may be in danger."

"Oh, boy." Diana rolled her eyes. She was losing patience with the class quickly.

"How many of you walk, jog, or bike?" Matt asked.

The whole class, probably close to twenty women, raised their hands.

"I'll bet there are many times when you're on one of the trails alone." Matt stood, feet apart in a wide stance, his hands steepled. "While our community is very safe, it's better to have someone with you. Walk or bike with a friend. If you don't have someone who can go along, at least consider going at times of the day when the trails are busy."

He continued with admonitions for staying safe by making good choices. I thought to myself if I were someone who made good choices, the man in my life would not have decided I needed a "Be Safe" women's self-defense class as a Valentine's Day gift. (He'd also gifted me with a hefty contribution to the Laguna Beach ARL in my name and beautiful emerald earrings. Did the guy know me or what?) He'd given Diana the same. Well, not the earrings but the contribution and the self-defense class.

And so, here we were.

Next, Matt covered what he called "verbal self-defense" which meant things you could say to calm a potentially threatening state of affairs. I was all for using words instead of violence and he did a great job of explaining body language, verbal cues, and danger signs. The problem was really reading the person and knowing whether they would respond to attempts to be calmed. If they weren't on drugs or not truly intent on killing you, you probably stood a chance.

"If you use these techniques, you may not have to use physical force." Matt continued. "Even if your attacker is much bigger than you."

"For instance, what if I approached this lady?" He moved in a menacing stance toward Betty. "What could she do to defuse and defend?"

"I tell you what I'd do." Betty's voice carried from the front. "I'd knee you in your boy parts and make a run for it." She demonstrated with a raised knee and, judging from the expression on Matt's face, she'd made contact.

"Let's take a short break," he croaked.

After the break, Betty was escorted to the back row by one of the helpers. Back where Diana and I had chosen to station ourselves.

"Hello, girls." Betty shifted her purse to her other arm and held out a hand decorated with bright blue polish. "I'm Betty Foxx."

"Nice manicure," I noted.

"It's from the Bow Wow Boutique. It's paw-lish, spelled p-a-w, paw. I figure if I'm gonna sell the products, I should use them."

Diana started to say something, but ended up with a polite cough. She seemed awestruck by Betty's drawn-on eyebrows which were artfully painted on—and not with a beauty product intended for eyebrows. It looked like she'd used orange lipstick, but maybe it was another Bow Wow Boutique item she was trying out.

Betty pointed a blue-tipped finger at Diana "You have a dog?"

"Several," Diana answered.

"We sell a lot of this stuff." Betty turned her fingers this way and that. "I don't get it, but who am I to say? I've got a job. Melanie's a nice boss."

"Melinda," I corrected without thinking.

She swiveled my direction. "I don't think I caught your name."

Diana made the intro. "Betty, meet Carolina Lamont."

"Holy dog farts, you're the cousin what's always stealing Cookie's brooch." Her lipstick eyebrows went up an inch. "She was fit to be tied last time you took it."

"My brooch." I corrected.

"Uh-uh." Betty shook her head. "You got it with you?" She looked around like Grandma Tillie's brooch might be somewhere in plain sight where she could snatch it for Melinda.

"Of course not," I replied. "It's somewhere even Mel can't get to it."

"Well, where is it?" She was a persistent cross-examiner.

"Oh, look." I pointed. "I think Matt wants to get started again."

The second part of the class went quickly, with Matt and his assistants demonstrating escape moves. He promised next week we'd get into more of the defensive moves.

"That was fun, girls." Betty retrieved her shiny black patent-leather purse from the floor and joined Diana and me. She'd kept it on her arm for most of the class, and then finally had given in and parked it firmly between her feet. "When my daughter signed me up for this 'Be Safe' deal, I thought it would be boring, but I was wrong. See you next week."

And with that, the little pajama-clad lady race-walked herself out of the room.

I looked at Diana. She looked at me. We burst out laughing.

"Well, bless her heart, she's an original." I grinned.

I wasn't sure where Mel had found Betty Foxx, but the woman was an absolute hoot.

Chapter Ten

I CHUCKLED ABOUT Betty and her pajamas as I got dressed the next morning.

Maybe it would simplify life for us all if we just wore our pj's all day. Though I didn't think my oversized P.U.P. (Protecting Unwanted Pets) T-shirt and plaid shorts had quite the same flair as Betty's leopard-print loungewear and pearls.

Malone had left a message on my cell phone letting me know I could come by the police station and pick up Grandma Tillie's brooch.

Apparently, he and the investigative team had decided my grandmother's brooch had nothing to do with the stabbing. Go figure, huh?

I was relieved they were releasing it. I knew my cousin, Mel, would have a difficult time breaking into police evidence to swipe it, but I'd feel so much better when it was back in my possession.

And, of course, now she had Pajama Betty on the lookout for it as well.

Not one to let any grass grow under my feet, I headed over to the Laguna Beach PD right away.

A short trip from my office, the Laguna Beach police department was located in a row of brick buildings in the downtown area. City Hall, the PD and the Fire Department were co-located in the complex.

There was an information desk as you entered the lobby and I approached it. Two familiar faces glanced up.

Sally looked up and greeted me. "Hi, Caro," Small and trim, she looked harmless but make no mistake, the lady could hold her own.

"Hey, how's our favorite pet shrink?" Lorraine, taller and tougher in appearance, turned from the desk where she was sorting papers.

"I'm doing well. How are you, and how is Buster?" Buster was her new Pug. He was a sweetheart of a dog.

"He's great. I'm so glad to have him."

We were on a first-name basis because we'd gotten to know each other when Diana had been falsely accused of murder, and had spent some time locked up in the Laguna Beach pokey. I know it's hard to picture, but Diana's one of a kind, and believe me, it had been a one-of-a-kind experience.

"Is Detective Malone in?" I asked. "He's expecting me."

"Sure, go on back." Sally gestured. "You know where his office is."

Unfortunately, I did. I didn't really want to examine too closely the fact I had more than a passing knowledge of the location of the Laguna Beach Homicide Division's office.

I slipped through the door beside the front desk and walked the hallway to Malone's office which was just the hole in the wall I remembered. He was on the phone, but gestured for me to take a seat.

I perched on the edge of the folding chair across from him.

"Yes." His face was taut, and his body language said he wasn't thrilled with what he was hearing on the other end of the line. "Yes, I understand."

He ended the call by putting down the receiver with a snap. I wondered if he'd learned the technique from my mama. Not quite slamming down the phone. It was a click. But with enough force that it communicated the disgust, the irritation, the I-am-done-talking-to-you-now finality. It was a skill and a talent.

Until this minute, I'd only been on the receiving end of the click; I'd never actually seen it done.

I raised my gaze from the desk phone to the detective behind the desk. His handsome face was expressionless. Judd Malone would make a great poker player. He leaned back in the chair, his posture relaxed and body language neutral. The only "tell" betraying his frustration was the tap of his pen.

He was obviously not having a good day. I'd just pick up my property and give him his space.

"I came for my brooch."

He made eye contact, his steely blue gaze unwavering.

"My grandma's brooch," I prompted. "You called me."

"I don't have it."

"What do you mean?" I scooted forward so fast I almost fell off the folding chair. "You lost it?"

"No, the Feds have it." He tossed the papers he held onto the desk. Again, a lot of disgust in the action. Really, he and Mama Kat had it down.

"What?"

"The investigation is now a federal case. The Feds have taken all the evidence. I am off the case."

"The Feds have my brooch?"

He nodded. "It's safe, Caro. They'll return it when their CSIs are done going through all the evidence."

"Excuse me, Detective! The Feds have Grandma Tillie's brooch?" I knew I was sort of shrieking by now, but you know what? I didn't care.

"Yep." Malone leaned forward in his chair. "The Feds have your grandma's brooch and my murder investigation."

He didn't shriek, but from the thunderclouds behind his eyes, I could tell he would have if it wouldn't ruin his tough cop image.

"Who do I need to talk to?" I would call them up and let them know I'd be expecting my property returned right away.

"That was FBI field agent John Milner." Malone pointed at the phone. "I believe you two have met. Would you like Agent Milner's number?" He jotted the info on a scrap of paper and extended it to me.

I snatched the note and rose to leave. "Agent Milner will be hearing from me."

"I'm sure he will." I got the impression he thought Milner deserved the grief.

I hurried from the office before Malone could think to mention how I was dressed the last time he'd seen me.

I TRIED THE number Detective Malone had given me before I headed to my first appointment of the day.

Voicemail. Great. I left a message.

My message was no-nonsense, but my face burned as I realized he'd undoubtedly connect the name I'd left with the crazy jet-haired chick in the skimpy outfit from the other night.

I could not believe Grandma Tillie's brooch was now out of reach in Federal evidence. It was one thing when it was locked up a few blocks away and in the possession of Detective Malone. But now in federal evidence?

Bizarre. Ridiculous. Unacceptable.

Turning the Mercedes onto Laurel Canyon Road, I took some deep breaths. It was just a piece of jewelry. True, it was a family heirloom and important to me, but, seriously, no one had died.

It was safe where it was, and I would get it back. It was simply going to take a little longer.

The good news was even though I didn't have the brooch, neither did my cousin, Mel.

Chapter Eleven

YOU'VE PROBABLY heard the adage about people looking like their pets.

I have to say, in all the years I've been involved in pet therapy, while there are cases where that may be true, there are just as many where you wonder at some of the more incongruent pairings.

Take my cousin, Melinda. Tall, elegant, and gorgeous. Yet Mel's canine, Missy, is a crown-wearing, title-carrying, Ugliest Bulldog.

No offense, Missy-girl, it's just a fact.

And take my friend, Diana. She's nothing if not glamorous perfection. But her puggle, Mr. Wiggles, is far from perfection. The rescue pug-beagle mix was the sweetest dog ever, but a non-regulation ear and an underbite did not make for a glam dog.

And then there's my next client, Matt Bjarni, the big russet-haired bodybuilder guy from our self-defense class. He'd called after learning from some other attendees that I worked with problem pets.

Matt was the owner of the tiniest foo-foo puppy you've ever seen. Chachi is a teacup Maltese that tips the cuteness scale at way beyond cute. On the weight scale—well, let's just say soaking wet, Chachi might be all of two pounds.

Matt had called me about Chachi, and we'd decided to meet at the dog park today, because the little pooch was having problems with— get this—being aggressive with other dogs. The Laguna Beach dog park is separated into two distinct areas with a large running area for big dogs and a smaller area for the medium to small to tiniest dogs. The small-dog side even had a bit of shade which was welcome on this blue-sky, warmer-than-normal Southern California day.

Matt was already there with Chachi protectively cradled in his arms. I sat down beside them on the bench. Chachi was so adorable and so incredibly tiny. Matt's massive forearms were bigger around than she was, and little bits of white fur stuck out between the fingers of his big beefy hands.

"Let's put her down and see how she does, okay?" I'd intervene if there was a problem, but I needed to see her in action to understand the problem.

Matt reluctantly placed Chachi on the ground.

The little white ball of fluff shivered a bit and then began to sniff around. The farther she got from our spot on the bench, the braver she became, straightening her stance and pouncing on blades of grass. The Maltese breed is generally playful and was once considered a sort of royal dog. "Ye ancient Dogge of Malta" as they were once called, originated in Malta, as you might expect from the name, but then Crusaders returning home from the Mediterranean brought them to England. The breed has been an aristocrat of the canine world for over twenty-eight centuries and recognized by the AKC since 1888.

Generally, a pretty easy breed. At the moment, there didn't seem to be any problem at all. At least, not one that was apparent. I wondered if there was something different in the environment when there'd been an issue.

Matt tensed as a group of three teen girls approached, their pocket puppies trailing behind. I recognized one of the girls, Erikka, with her long-haired Chihuahua named Livi Tyler. I didn't know the other two girls.

Matt reached down to pick up Chachi as the group got closer, but I stopped him with a touch. "Let's see how she does."

The dogs picked up speed and raced around the girls to greet Chachi. Livi, Erikka's girl, sniffed first, and then the other dog, a miniature Pinscher, bounded forward.

Pinschers have a distinctive gait, sort of a bounce. He also sniffed at Chachi without any reaction. Then the biggest, if you can use the word "big" in the context of these mini-pooches, raced up. A Yorkie-Poo, and though bigger than the other two—still probably no more than four pounds—she ran up, sniffed like the other two, and then barked right in Chachi's face.

Chachi's expression was haughty outrage, but she didn't back up. A low growl started in her throat and grew louder as the little Yorkie-Poo circled and barked once more.

Again, Matt moved to scoop her up and out of harm's way. As he did, she was distracted by his movement, and the other dogs looked his way as well. In zero seconds flat, Chachi was between Matt and the other dogs, and her short warning barks said, "Back off, girls, you're scaring my human."

Or at least that's how I interpreted it. It was clear to me the interaction was not so much about Chachi and the dogs, as it was about Matt. By being overprotective of Chachi, he'd actually made the situation unstable. Then, because he was worried and unsettled, the little dog reacted.

"Matt, let's try this. Lean back and let them sort it out," I said in a low voice.

I looked up at the girls. "Ladies, if you don't mind, can we leave the dogs a bit?" I kept my voice low.

The girls nodded.

"Erikka, I know Livi. What are the other pups' names?" Again, I kept my voice level.

"Freddie's my dog," The tall blond pointed to the miniature Pinscher.

"And Nina is mine." The dark-haired girl snapped her fingers, and Nina looked up.

"Hi, Nina. Hello, Freddie." The dogs tipped their heads and looked at me as they recognized their names.

"This little girl is Chachi." I made the introductions. "I'm Caro and this is my friend, Matt. We're working with Chachi on playing nice with friends."

"She's adorable." Erikka smiled.

"Thanks." Matt was still tense and barely looked up to acknowledge the girls. But he had leaned back, as I'd asked him to, and Chachi seemed a touch more stable.

It's often the case that the behavior is in some way related to the pet parent, and in this case, I thought Matt's worry about Chachi's safety had translated to her that it was an unsafe environment. Once he learned to chill out, she would, too.

I had a few small toys in my bag and pulled out some bright-colored balls. They were smaller than tennis balls and just the right size for the little dogs. The girls threw them, and the four pooches scampered off in chase. Soon, Chachi was joining in the play like one of the crowd.

The girls—I'm afraid I still didn't know all their names—moved out into the full sun, working on their tans, I imagined. Matt and I, both redheads and prone to burning, stayed in the shade.

We talked a little about what he could do to work with Chachi and get her more comfortable. I, as always, encouraged exercise. However, I suspected that he now realized his part in the unstable behavior, and that Chachi's problems with aggression were behind her.

I began to pack up my bag to leave.

"I understand you were at the Greyhound event where that guy was killed." Matt took a deep drink from his water bottle, his eyes still on his dog. "That must have been scary."

"It was a little scary," I admitted. "The man grabbed me just before he collapsed. Did you know him?"

"No, I didn't know him at all. Wasn't one of my fitness clients."

"I guess he was pretty new to the area. No one seems to know much about him."

"Do the police have any leads?"

I wasn't sure how much I was supposed to share, so I opted for vague. "I understand it's become a federal investigation and the FBI has taken over finding the killer. I hope they find him soon."

"Him? Do they know the killer was a man?" Matt leaned around me to keep his eyes on his dog.

"I don't think they've said, but I assumed it would be difficult for a woman to have enough strength to stab a good-sized guy with a carving knife."

"Not necessarily." Matt glanced my way and then went back to watching Chachi. "Though upper body strength has to be developed, there are many women with enough power to stab someone. Especially if there's an element of surprise."

"I guess you'll be showing us those kinds of things in the 'Be Safe' course?" I was surprised at myself, but I'd been looking forward to the next class.

I hadn't thought about the possibility of a female killer, but Matt had a good point. I hoped Mr. Agent-in-Charge Milner was looking at all possibilities. Maybe I could glean some information when he called me back about my brooch.

I said good-bye to Matt and checked my messages on the way to my car to see if Agent Milner had returned my call.

No dice. There was a call, however, from Blanche LeRue.

She wanted me to stop by the Greys Matter office and give her an update on the Greyhound owners I'd contacted. I was happy to do so, and I was ready with a question for Blanche.

IT WASN'T TOURIST season, but it was Saturday, so parking was at a premium in downtown Laguna. I circled several times before finally finding a spot near the building where the Greyhound rescue had their offices. It was in an older part of downtown, nestled between a tailor shop and a pottery store. The brick front appeared to be original, but the whole block had been updated. The streetscape in front sported fun brightly-painted flowerpots and wrought-iron benches that were spaced at intervals.

The front door had an outline of a graceful Greyhound and "Greys Matter" written in a flowing script.

As I reached for the handle, a dark-haired man in a green polo shirt and plaid golf pants pushed past me. His face was dark with anger, and he stomped to the curb where he hit the button on a key fob.

A yellow late-model Mercedes sedan answered. He yanked open the car door, got in, and slammed the door with such force I thought it might break the window.

Wowza. I could only hope he'd cool down before he took to driving in traffic, because he already had the "rage" part of the road rage equation.

I let myself into the Greys Matter office. The suite was nice, but not fancy. Large photos of Greyhounds lined the walls.

The breed really was an elegant one, and the photographer had captured their unique traits. When a Greyhound is in full stride, all four feet leave the ground. One of the photos captured this to full advantage. Each racing Greyhound is tattooed with their birth date in the right ear and their litter number in the left. Another photo was a close-up of a racer's ear, the tattooed numbers clearly visible—a photo that spoke to the story of these gentle dogs.

Blanche came out to meet me, looking much more like herself today in a dark blue jacket over a khaki-colored skirt. Her white blouse was crisply pressed and stain-free. She escorted me back to her large office. We passed two small offices and a boardroom on the way back.

"Thanks for stopping by, Caro." While she was more pulled together, Blanche seemed only a little less tense than the last time we'd talked. "I know you're busy with your regular clients. I really appreciate you working with our Greyhound parents."

"Who was the guy that just left?" I asked.

She didn't answer right away.

"I passed him as I came in," I prompted. I couldn't imagine she'd forgotten him. He seemed pretty memorable to me.

"Oh, that was George Thomas, our attorney."

"He seemed upset." Understatement of the year.

"A little disagreement over billable hours is all." She tried a smile that ended up more of a grimace.

"None of my business, but if that was a little disagreement, I'd hate to see a big disagreement."

"Oh, he'll be fine." She waved away my concern.

I looked around. Her office was, like her, sleek and efficient. It was free of clutter, the workspace was clear, and the few papers in sight neatly stacked.

"Are you the only full-time staff for Greys Matter?" I only knew a little about the rescue group and mostly second-hand, through Diana.

"Pretty much." She dropped into the leather desk chair. "Dave, who does the books, is part time. You know Dave, don't you? I think his firm's office is in your building."

I nodded. Dave didn't really have a "firm." There was just him and a desk, but I was sure his tax work paid well based on his wife, Alana's, baubles and penchant for designer togs.

"So, just you two?"

"And George, our attorney whom you passed as he was leaving, is on retainer. We have a volunteer who does our website. And other volunteers who serve various roles. Often, we have a volunteer out front, but not today. But that's not a problem. I can see the reception desk from here." She pointed out a curved mirror in the hallway which gave a clear view of the corridor and front office.

The small staff arrangement wasn't unusual. Many rescues use volunteers, which helps to keep their overhead down and allows them to do more for their cause.

I pulled out the spreadsheet Verdi had created and handed it to Blanche. "Here's the list you sent me of attendees who had dogs at the event."

"And are most of them willing to consult with you?" She ran one manicured index finger down the list.

"Some didn't see any need." I seated myself in one of the two chairs across from the desk. "Most are not reporting any problems, but were open to an evaluation. I've just begun working through the appointments."

"Are you familiar with file sharing?" she asked.

"Um, not really." I wasn't really sure what she meant.

"It would be useful because we could share this spreadsheet." She pointed at the paper. "You can update it and I can look at it online."

"Sounds like it would be helpful." I was amazed at Blanche's technical prowess.

"Just download this program." She jotted a note and handed it to me. "I'll send you the info we need in order to share documents."

"Great." I was all for using less paper.

"I am so happy you're doing this." She straightened in her chair and laid the list aside. Then picked it back up and then set it aside again.

"I'm happy to help."

"I had such hopes that the Fifty Shades fund-raiser would bring in some much-needed donations for the rescue. There are so many Greyhounds out there who need our help." Blanche hesitated, her lip quivering slightly. "So far, no one has asked for their money to be returned. I'm grateful for that."

I reached over and patted her hand. "I think they are all about helping the animals, and they understand the rescue organization had nothing to do with the problems."

"I hope you're right." She adjusted the collar on her jacket.

"Has anyone figured out how the rabbit got into the room?" I had to ask.

"*D'Orange Maison* tells me there had been a children's birthday party earlier in the room next door, and the magician's rabbit either got loose or someone opened the cage."

"Poor bunny." I could see the room again in my mind. Dogs running, people chasing, tables crashing.

"When you're ready to bill for these evaluations with the Greyhound owners," Blanche said, back to the business at hand, "please send the invoice to me directly. This is something I decided to do and not an expense the board approved."

"Certainly, I can do that." She'd already told me to bill her when we talked at her house, but I didn't remind her. With all the woman had on her plate between the murder, the disastrous fund-raiser, and now an angry attorney, it seemed like it would be enough to make anyone forgetful.

She rose, and I did too.

If I was to get to everyone today, I needed to keep moving.

"Have you heard anything about the investigation?" she asked as we continued down the hall toward the reception area. "Are they still looking for the young man who was part of the catering staff?"

"The only thing I know is that it's now a Federal investigation."

"What?" She stopped mid-stride. "Why would the Feds be involved?" She seemed shaken by the news.

"I don't know." There was still no one at the front desk, I noted. "It must have something to do with who the victim, Victor Lustig, really was."

Blanche had gone very quiet.

"Did you know that wasn't really his name?" I watched for a reaction.

"Hmm." She didn't say yes or no.

"You said you hadn't met him before that night at the fund-raiser, right?"

"Right." It was an affirmative, but one without a great deal of conviction.

"One of the clients I met with thought they'd seen him here at the office."

"Who said that?"

"I'm not sure." I wasn't going to point the finger at Marjory Whedon. It could be she'd misunderstood what her husband had said. Or it was possible Raymond Whedon was wrong about what he'd seen. In any case, I wasn't going to put them on the spot.

"Whoever it was must have been mistaken." Blanche ran her hands over the freshwater pearl necklace she wore as if it were a rosary.

"That could be." I hesitated, my hand on the door. "I'll keep you posted on my progress with the other Greyhound owners."

I walked to my car on autopilot, questions pinging in my head.

It was possible Raymond Whedon was mistaken.

However, given Blanche's reaction, it was also possible he was right and Victor, or whatever his real name was, had been at the Greys Matter office.

But why would Blanche insist he hadn't been there? Could he have come in when she wasn't in the office?

I didn't know why Blanche wouldn't want to admit to having previously met the dead guy.

But one thing I knew for sure about Blanche's denial was, as Grandma Tillie used to say, "That dog don't hunt."

Chapter Twelve

DOGBERT WAS A morning person.

I, however, was not. It took me a little wake-up time and a Texas-sized serving of caffeine to face the day. I started the coffee while Dog waited patiently at the door for his morning trip around the neighborhood. He was quiet, but his perky ears and his ready stance said, "Are you coming?"

I took a peek outside. The sun was just barely reaching finger rays over the hills, so it might be a little chilly. I grabbed a sweatshirt and Dogbert's leash and walked out into the crisp salt-air morning.

Verdi's car wasn't in the driveway next door. I was surprised she was gone so early, but what with working two jobs—at the Koffee Klatch and as our receptionist—the girl's day undoubtedly started early.

I clipped Dogbert's leash to his collar and, as we reached the sidewalk, Verdi's little green Fiat pulled in and she got out. Her backpack was slung over one shoulder and she had a paper bag and two cups of coffee in her hands. She must need even more caffeine than I did.

"'Morning," I called.

Her head jerked up. "Ah—good morning."

"Sorry, I didn't mean to startle you. Do you—" I was going to ask if she needed help, but she skittered into the house.

Verdi was usually very chatty, especially since she'd been helping out next door with April Mae's cats, but she must have been pressed for time.

Dogbert moved at a fast clip through the neighborhood. I hoped Verdi wasn't still feeling regret about getting me to recommend her brother to Dino for catering help. I was absolutely sure she had no way of knowing what would transpire at the ill-fated fund-raiser. I also hoped she wasn't feeling bad about the trip down Crazy Street that had led us to dress up as video game characters and almost get arrested.

I shrugged. She probably had to get ready for work. I'd catch up with her later.

Dogbert and I finished our walk in no time. A little too soon for Dog, who would have liked a bit more time to stop and smell the roses. And the bushes, and the trees, and the mailboxes, and . . . well, you get the picture. Back home, I showered, dressed, and grabbed my list for the day. Unlike Blanche, I'm a pen and paper kind of gal and an in-hand list helps me tame the day if I know what's ahead.

I checked it quickly, grabbed my Coach tote and headed to the garage. I'd left the top down on the Mercedes when I'd pulled it into the garage last night, and the forecast indicated I could leave it down.

When I pulled out of the garage, I noted Verdi's car was again gone. She sure drank coffee fast. I turned toward Pacific Coast Highway and my first appointment of the day.

The Pacific sparkled with the promise of a blue-sky day, and I didn't mind the stop-and-go traffic because I got a chance to enjoy the morning sun.

Even with the traffic, it took very little time to arrive at Diamond Cove. I pulled up to the guard shack. Although I'm not sure you would want to use the term "shack" in describing a checkpoint cottage as large as many southern California homes, and boasting technology that rivaled most corporate campuses.

The guard himself was right out of Hollywood casting. I presented my driver's license to him so he could verify my name was on the visitor list. I'm all for safety, but with this much security, you've got to ask yourself what on earth people are keeping out or keeping in. Once I'd been verified, he came around and put a key in the gate and pushed the button to lift the arm. I drove through and headed to the last house on the street as I'd been instructed.

If the guard had been from central casting, Alice and Robert Tiburon's home looked like something from a James Bond movie. White and sleek, it perched at the edge of a cliff like a giant sea creature. My taste ran more toward the traditional, but I could appreciate the beauty of the architecture which was iconic SoCal modern.

As I approached the frosted glass front door, it slid open soundlessly, and a lovely older woman greeted me.

"You must be Ms. Lamont." She smiled. "We're expecting you."

"Yes, I am, but please call me Caro." I glanced around the

entryway. It was also a bit futuristic for me, but the lines were beautiful. As I suspected, the floor plan was open to take the best advantage of an incredible view. The house had been designed in such a way that the ocean seemed like an accessory, complementing the other furnishings.

"If you'll come with me, I'll take you to Jorene." She motioned for me to follow.

I wasn't sure who Jorene was, but I was glad to have an escort, and I hoped someone would be along for the return trip, because I didn't think I could find my way back to the front door if my life depended on it. The twists and turns we took through the house guaranteed I'd be lost for sure.

"Here we are." My guide stopped in an alcove off another full living area. The room was filled with dog paraphernalia. A curly-haired woman dressed in cargo shorts rose from the floor where she'd been rubbing the tummy of an ebony-furred fellow.

"I'm Jorene." She brushed her palm on her shorts and then held it out.

"Caro Lamont." I shook her hand. A good strong handshake. "You're the dogs' trainer?"

Nothing had been mentioned about Jorene in the notes Verdi had provided, just that the Tiburons would like their dogs checked out.

"Not really," the woman explained. "I take care of the dogs—diet, exercise, vet appointments, etc."

Ah, a dog nanny.

"This guy is Duke, and Sleeping Beauty over there is Lady." She indicated a white Greyhound napping on the couch.

"How long have the Tiburons had the dogs?"

"I believe about three years." Jorene reached down and patted Duke. "I've been here two."

"Do they spend time with Duke and Lady?"

I knew it was none of my business. Most of my wealthy clients had pets because they loved animals and enjoyed the companionship. But not all, so I couldn't help asking.

I understood there were different levels of animal love. Not everyone was like Diana. And as long as the dogs weren't neglected, they were having a good life. Still, they're such loyal and loving creatures, they deserve to get love in return.

"They do." Her short answer said I should back off.

Right. None of my business. I tamped down my bristle. I was here to check on the dogs, not to pass judgment.

"Any change in behavior since the fund-raiser?" I went through my usual questions about anxiety indicators such as appetite, personality, or other changes.

"Nothing." Jorene shook her brunette locks. "As I said, they're such sweet dogs."

"That's great." I sat down on the floor by Duke and visited a little while longer with Jorene who clearly loved the dogs to pieces. Soon, Lady joined us and we did a little throw-the-ball playtime.

I'd accomplished what I'd come for and needed to move on to my next appointment, so I got to my feet and thanked Jorene for her time.

"Would you mind very much walking me out?" I asked. "I'm afraid I wasn't paying close enough attention to the route we took to get here."

"No problem." Jorene gathered some of the dog toys and dropped them in a basket by the couch. "I used to get lost a lot when I first started."

She led me back through the house and to the front door—a shorter distance than I'd realized. Unlike many of the clients I worked with, there were no dog toys strewn about. Perhaps Duke and Lady were kept to their own area. Again, not my business.

"There you go." She walked me to the front door. "Thanks for your information about the dogs."

"You're welcome." Just as I reached the door, it opened and Alice Tiburon stepped through. I'd only talked to her at the Greyhound event for a brief moment, but she was memorable.

Striking, if not beautiful. Today, she wore a business suit rather than an evening gown, but the silver streaks in her hair were drawn out by the silver threads running through the tweed knit. The jacket had a wide zipper, and the pencil skirt accented her height and slenderness.

"Oh." She slid to a stop in her black stilettos. "Who are you?"

"Caro Lamont."

"Oh, the dog person." The deep contralto I remembered from the night of the Greyhound event was dismissive. She stepped past me. "They are fine, I assume."

"They seem great. Jorene does a really wonderful job taking care of them."

"Oh, yes." She abruptly become aware of Jorene, as if surprised by her presence. "Thank you. You can go."

The dog nanny slipped away.

Alice leaned back, crossed her arms, and looked at me. "Sorry to rush, but I've got to grab some papers and get back to the office." She flashed a pinched smile. "Nice to meet you."

"If you have just a moment," I said to her back. I wasn't the slip-away type.

She turned. "Yes?"

"You're on the Grey Matters board, right?"

She nodded. "I'm the Chair."

"The man who was killed, had you met him before? Maybe even seen him at the Greys Matter office?"

Blanche hadn't actually suggested I ask about the dead guy. I had the impression what Blanche really cared about was whether anyone was so upset by the murder they would pull their support of the rescue group. I thought asking about the dead guy was a good place to start. The loss of Alice Tiburon's support would be a huge hit for Greys Matter.

"No." Alice left it at a one-syllable response.

She tugged at the zipper of her jacket and pulled the edge down, smoothing it against her tiny waist. I waited for her to go on. She didn't.

"If you need anything, I've left my card with Jorene."

She opened her mouth and then closed it. Then with a sigh she asked, "Was there anything else?"

"No, just let me know if the dogs begin to exhibit any signs of anxiety."

"Of course," she said. "Thank you again." She walked away before I was out the door.

Mama Kat would have been appalled.

I'd seen that kind of abruptness before in high-powered women. For that matter, even the Texas pageant crowd had its share of no-time-for-the-niceties women. I couldn't remember what Alice Tiburon did professionally, but it must play well in her world because it appeared she and her husband were doing just fine for themselves.

My next stop was another Greyhound owner on the list, and then I had a stop at Ruby Point to check in with Ollie Hembry and a problem he was having with a new addition to his pack. Ollie had a menagerie of mutts at his place, but, like Diana, he was always open to fostering another if there was a need.

I checked out with the guard and turned toward Pacific Coast

Highway again, back to Laguna proper. I checked the address and headed up into the hills. I loved my house in The Village. Perfect size for me, awesome view, and minutes from my office. Still as I drove the steep road to the TOW, that's Top of the World for those of you who aren't local, I have to admit I fantasized just a little about life at the top.

The house where my next stop was scheduled was unlike the one I'd just come from. This house in the hills was a nice home and had a beautiful view, but beyond that, was much like the properties in my neighborhood.

The Greyhound owners were happy to see me and had some questions about their brindle hound. They had little to say about the incident at the fund-raiser. They'd been near their dog and had been able to get her calmed down quickly. We talked through some chewing issues. I believed them to be separation anxiety-related and provided some tips to deal with the issue. Greyhounds are people lovers and can be stressed by their people leaving.

The trick is to figure out what works for each individual dog. There are conditioning techniques that are often successful. I provided a list and suggested they experiment and keep track of which things worked best. I promised to check back and see how they were doing.

Once again, I left my card with the Greyhound owners and was off to visit Ollie. We'd met when a client of mine and his next-door neighbor had been killed. Since then, had become friends.

The man at the Ruby Point guard shack had me sign in, but he recognized me as I was a frequent visitor. I drove past Diana's house to Ollie Hembry's. The issue he'd called me about concerned Morkie, his Lhasa Apso and Poodle mix. She'd been part of a group of dogs rescued from a puppy mill, and he was fostering her. She'd bonded with Ollie, but was refusing to let the groomer touch her.

As I may have mentioned before, Ollie doesn't leave the house. He's a victim of agoraphobia. The Divine Dog Spa was the go-to grooming place in town, but Ollie couldn't go there. He needed someone to come to him. I'd recommended Kendall, a friend of mine, who I knew would be gentle with the dog and the owner.

I parked in front of Ollie's and picked up my bag as well as a batch of gluten-free dog treats I'd brought along. I often made dog treats to take to appointments as an icebreaker. Because Ollie had such a brood, it would be a great place to try my latest recipe, though I always had to remind Ollie the biscuits were for the dogs.

I rang the doorbell, and "God Save the Queen" filled the air. Unlike the visit at Diamond Cove and the Tiburon residence, Ollie answered the door himself, with dark sunglasses, long black hair, black jeans, and black T-shirt. I'd never seen him in anything else. I pictured a whole closet full of replicas lined up and ready.

"Hello, luv." Ollie gave me a hug. "You're looking especially smashing today."

I pushed my unruly red locks out of my eyes and glanced down at my unremarkable black jeans and loose Elie Tahari blouse, which had looked fine when I'd left home that morning. But after I'd rolled around on the floor with Greyhounds and Greyhound parents, it left a lot to be desired. Maybe it was the all-black look Ollie identified with.

"Thank you," I said. "You look smashing yourself."

"Better than smashed, eh, luv?"

"Right." I smiled at his attempt at humor. "Much better. Now where's this little guy who's giving you trouble?"

We walked into Ollie's living room, which always reminded me of a castle with its opulence and heavy ornate furniture. Don't get me wrong, it's gorgeous but not my taste. To each his or her own, right? The modern Tiburon mansion had not been my cup of tea either. In addition to the contrast in styles, unlike the ultra-modern Tiburon mansion, Ollie's living area was not free of dog paraphernalia. I stepped over a trail of chew toys, colorful balls, and plush toys as I walked through.

"Here's the little troublemaker." Ollie gently picked up the cutest Lhasa-Poo I've ever seen. He cuddled the little white dog against his chest and the dog licked his chin. "The wee doggie was a bit poorly when Diana brought her to me, but she's better now."

"Aww, she's adorable." I didn't immediately touch the pup. "Hi, Morkie."

"She's a tad wonky. The vet did a scan, and she may have some brain damage or even eye problems." He gently patted the bit of fluff. "Like to get my hands on those bloody berks . . . ," Ollie didn't finish the sentence but he didn't have to.

With puppy mills, those types of injuries usually meant the dog was abused. I wasn't sure about the term Ollie'd used, but I had several names of my own for people who hurt animals.

"She looks healthy, Ollie. You've done a good job."

"At first I couldn't put a collar on her." He laid the dog carefully in the dog bed. "She would just scream. Eerie sound, that. Almost like a human cry."

"You said she can't tolerate the groomer?"

"No. Jade sent someone by, and it was total shambles."

Jade was the head groomer at the Divine Dog Spa and would have been sensitive to Ollie's situation as well as a dog with special needs.

"Let's talk about how the visit went." I encouraged him to step me through the details.

We talked about the incident, and I suggested a series of behavior modifications with rewards to get Morkie to tolerate being groomed. It could be a slow process and would take patience. But Ollie had a lot of patience and time on his hands.

Ollie had heard about the stabbing at the Fifty Shades of Greyhound event and had lots of questions. I told him what I knew, and, to my surprise, he knew Verdi's brother.

"Sharp kid, Eugene," he pronounced. "Helped me with some computer problems. He ran with a dodgy crowd, though, as kids will. I think he got himself straightened out. Who am I to pass judgment, you know?"

I did know. Ollie had a checkered past himself, which was why he lived alone in this big house with only the dogs for company. His wife had gotten fed up with the drugs and drinking. One day, she'd taken the kids and moved back to England. At least, according to the word around town. Ollie himself never talked about his family.

We wrapped up, and I left Ollie with some notes and promised to call Jade with recommendations for when Kendall came to groom Morkie. Kendall was always gentle with the dogs, and once he understood the process, he would do fine. Maybe I'd just talk to him directly.

I grabbed lunch and spent the afternoon at the office updating files. I also made notes for Blanche on which Greyhound owners I'd talked with already and anything else they'd shared.

By the time I'd finished my day and headed for home, it was dusk, and, in Ollie's words, I was "knackered"."

Which, for those of you this side of the pond, means dead-dog tired.

Chapter Thirteen

SUNSET IS LAGUNA Beach's best feature.

Not that the coastal village isn't beautiful on a perfect weather day like today had been. But sunset in Laguna is nothing short of phenomenal—almost every time.

I turned into my driveway and hit the button for the garage door opener. I hesitated as I did. There was a light on next door. Maybe Verdi was spending the night.

April Mae had told her she was welcome to stay at the house, but Verdi had her apartment and most nights stayed there. She took great care of April Mae's cats, Tobey and Minou, which was the most important thing.

I hadn't noticed her car, so she could have accidently left a light on when she'd left. Not a big deal, and, if that was the case, I could run next door and turn it off after dinner.

I parked my car in the garage and pushed the button to close the door.

Dogbert was thrilled to see me. Thelma and Louise barely acknowledged me. They lifted their furry heads as if to say, "Oh, it's you. Let us know when dinner is ready."

I took Dogbert for a quick walk and then back home changed into my most comfy clothes. Remember those yoga clothes I wore to the self-defense class? Yeah, those were the ones.

Note to self: must shop for something nicer before next week's class.

I fed my fur kids and started dinner for myself. As I threw together the spinach salad and tossed some toasted almonds on top, I considered the day. Pretty productive. My regular client load was under control. A few more Greyhound clients to go.

Maybe I'd have some news on Grandma Tillie's brooch tomorrow. That FBI agent still had not called me back.

Bloody berk. I used Ollie's term in my head. I still didn't know the meaning, but his tone had conveyed the gist.

I took my salad and a glass of Chardonnay out to my patio.

The light was still on next door at April Mae's house, and it bugged me. I couldn't tell for sure which light was on. It didn't appear to be the veranda. There was an enclosed veranda at the back of the house that had been set up as an area for Toby and Minou, April Mae's cats.

They'd become April Mae's cats in my mind. My next-door neighbor Kitty had named them, but when she was killed (another murder, I'm afraid) and her sister inherited the cats and the home, the two Bengal cats had immediately bonded with April Mae. I hoped she was faring well in getting things sorted out in her home state of Missouri. I missed her flamboyant presence.

I'd run next door as soon as I'd finished eating. If Verdi was there, I'd update her on the status of the investigation as I knew it. If she wasn't, I'd turn off the light in the house. Better than worrying about it all night.

I carried my dishes back inside, rinsed them and set them aside. I grabbed my sweatshirt, cell phone, and my key to the house next door just in case Verdi wasn't there. I stepped outside. There was no little green car in the drive, but I rang the doorbell anyway.

I unlocked the door and stepped in. The light I'd seen from my house was in the kitchen. Halfway down the hallway, I heard something. Maybe Verdi was there after all.

I could see a shadow moving in the kitchen.

"Verdi?" I called.

The shadow froze.

Okay, not Verdi.

I backed up, my eyes glued to the doorway, ready to turn and run if necessary.

A head popped around the corner.

I choked back a scream as I recognized the face. "Eugene?"

"Yes." He had on loose-fitting pajamas and clutched a bowl heaped with ice cream. I knew I should be afraid of, or at the very least cautious of, a "person-of-interest" in a murder investigation, but it was difficult to take seriously a baby-faced dude in flannel Star Wars jammies with a spoon full of Rocky Road halfway to his mouth.

"You know the police are looking for you?" Of course he did, but I had to say it anyway.

"Um, yeah." His eyes, so much like Verdi's, were round with fear.

I heard the door behind me open and turned to see Verdi walk in, her arms weighed down with grocery bags.

"Caro." Guilt washed her face. "I . . . uh . . . I," she stuttered.

"Go put the groceries in the kitchen, and then we need to talk." I moved so she could pass. "You, too." I pointed at Eugene who'd stuck the spoon in his bowl for another bite of ice cream.

I settled myself on the couch in April Mae's living room and waited for the brother and sister. I could hear furtive whispers but couldn't quite make out the conversation. Toby and Minou, the two Bengal cats, joined me on the couch, and I stroked their dappled coats as I waited.

I was giving Verdi and her brother a few minutes more and then I was done cooling my heels. I'd gone from scared out of my wits to fuming in the last few minutes, and I was ready to hear what the two of them had to say for themselves. Only a buzzard feeds on his friends, and, I have to tell you, I was feeling plenty picked on.

Finally, Verdi and Eugene appeared. They sat down facing me, straight-backed and nervous.

They looked so young and so dang scared my anger dissipated.

I would start with him. "Eugene, you know the police want to talk to you, right?"

He nodded.

"And, Verdi, you could be in a lot of trouble for hiding him instead of letting Detective Malone know he's here."

"I know." Verdi held steady eye contact. "But, Caro, he didn't kill that guy. The guy wasn't even who he claimed to be."

"Verdi—" Eugene's voice held a warning tone.

"So, who was he?" I knew from my conversation with Davis Pinter that the name he'd used was fictitious, but it didn't explain why he'd needed a phony name.

"He is—um—was Dirk Pennick," Eugene said. "A criminal and a con man. He was in prison at the same time as me. When I saw him at the event, I knew he was up to something. Probably figured a big deal like that, there'd be a lot of people with lot of money."

"Why didn't you tell someone about him?"

"I was going to tell Dino and let him have the people in charge throw Dirk out." Eugene swallowed hard. "I knew no one would believe me, but Dino's respected. They'd believe him."

"So why didn't you tell Dino?"

"I was looking for Dino, but then somebody stabbed Dirk, and everyone was hunting for me." His arms flailed as he talked. "They'd already decided I did it. I knew no one would hear me out. They didn't before. I have a record now, and it would be right back to jail for me."

Verdi sat quietly, her face frozen in place as Eugene told his story.

I leaned forward to talk to her. "Verdi, you—"

She stopped me. "Caro, you can't call the police." Her chin raised in defiance.

I turned back to her brother. "Eugene, did you stab Dirk?"

"No. Not that anyone cares." Cynicism tainted his answer.

"I don't want to hear that. Your sister obviously cares."

"Yeah." He looked at Verdi sheepishly.

"So, here are our options. I can call the police, and they'll come very quickly. I know, I've had them respond. Or I can call Detective Malone, and you, Verdi, can explain that your brother is here and would like to talk to him." I looked from one to the other. "Verdi, you know Malone He's fair."

She nodded and looked at her brother. "Eugene, I know you're scared. I'm scared, too. But, I think we should talk to the detective."

Eugene started to say something but then fell back in the chair, and the fight went out of him. "Okay, Sis."

I pulled my cell phone from my sweatshirt pocket and dialed Malone's number.

He answered right away. "Need help with the FBI again?" I guess the caller ID must have given away who was on the other end of the line.

"No." I hadn't needed help before, but this wasn't the time to go into that. "I'm at April Mae's house with Verdi, and she has something to tell you."

I handed the phone to Verdi, and she began her explanation. I turned to Eugene and said, "You might want to change clothes before Detective Malone arrives."

"What?" He looked down at the scattered droids on his dark blue flannel pj's. "Oh, right." He stood and shuffled down the hall, the pajama pants baggy on his skinny hips. "I'll be right back."

Verdi pushed the button to end the call with Malone and handed my phone back to me. "He's on his way." She looked around. "Where's Eugene?"

"He went to change his clothes." I tucked the phone back in my pocket.

"Probably a good idea." Verdi smiled slightly for the first time since she'd arrived. "He's always had a thing for sci-fi movies."

In what seemed like only seconds, there was a knock at the door. I got up and answered it.

"Caro." Malone was attired in his usual uniform of dark jeans, dark T-shirt, and leather jacket.

I wished I'd thrown on something other than yoga pants and a sweatshirt. Seemed Malone often got to see me at my worst.

"Verdi." He acknowledged my nervous burgundy-haired friend who stood wringing her hands. "I see you two are not in costume tonight." A smile lurked, but didn't quite break through.

I didn't appreciate the ribbing, but I did welcome his effort to lighten the tension.

"Your brother contacted you?" He got straight to the point.

"Yes, he did, detective." Verdi's voice shook. "He was afraid to come forward because of his record. But he didn't kill that guy," she finished in a stronger tone.

"I see." Malone stood, his feet planted apart. The cats moved to greet him, rubbing their regal heads against his legs. "I'd like to hear the story from him. Where is he?"

"He went to change clothes," I explained.

"I'll go get him." Verdi seemed relieved to move. "He's in the guest room." She hurried down the hall.

"Can't stay out of my murder investigations can you, Caro?" Malone shifted his gaze to me.

"Wow, we're on a first name basis?" I couldn't resist. "Why sugar, I think I must be growing on you."

"Seems to me Verdi wouldn't turn in her brother on her own." Malone rubbed his chin. "How did you figure out he was here?"

"A light was on," I admitted. "I came over to check it out."

"I hear the Greyhound lady has you visiting all the people who had dogs at the fancy dinner."

"That's right."

Where had he heard about my arrangement with Blanche?

"If you hear anything, I expect you to let me know." His blue eyes pinned me.

"Of course."

Verdi came back down the hall, her eyes wide and her face pale.

"Verdi, are you okay?" I stepped forward and grabbed her hands. "What is it?"

She pressed her lips together, swallowed and finally choked out, "Eugene is gone."

Chapter Fourteen

DETECTIVE MALONE raced around April Mae's house like a crazed rodeo clown being chased by a bull.

Though I didn't think he'd appreciate the clown comparison, I'd have to say I've never seen him move so fast. He'd pulled the gun that'd been hidden by the leather jacket, and he dashed down the hallway, feet pounding, slamming open every door.

He checked the bathrooms, the bedroom, the closets, and the guest room where Eugene had been staying. He had us show him the back door and then he searched the backyard, all the while on the phone requesting assistance.

Two uniformed officers arrived within minutes, and Malone was in full cop mode. He sent them off to search the backyard again and the surrounding neighborhood.

He made us repeat—several times—the information Eugene had shared about Victor aka Dirk. I thought Eugene had said Dirk Pen-something, and Verdi thought he'd said Dirk Ben-something. Neither of us were sure about the name, but, hey, we hadn't planned to have to repeat the information word for word to Detective Malone. We'd expected Eugene would give his own firsthand account.

"Tell me again what he said about what this guy did." Malone's voice was tight.

I looked over at Verdi. She sat cross-legged on the couch and twirled her hair with one finger. Her whole small being sagged against the cushions. The corners of her eyes drooped with exhaustion. I would take this round.

"Eugene said Dirk was a con man." I said, for what had to be the hundredth time.

"Which would make sense," I continued, "because the alias he chose to use was the guy who sold the Eiffel Tower to several people. Did you know the real Victor Lustig not only swindled people into thinking they were buying the Eiffel Tower, he also conned Al Capone?" I'd done my due diligence and looked him up after Davis

Pinter had pointed out the phony name.

"I'm aware." Malone's blue eyes were so dilated they looked black.
Okay, so not a good time for a history lesson.

The doorbell rang. "You two stay put." Malone jabbed his finger
at us.

It was the two officers he'd sent to check the neighborhood.
"Nothing. Do you want us to go door to door?"

"Nah." Malone shook his head. "He won't stick around here.
Make sure the night crew is on the watch for him though."

Verdi jumped up abruptly and pushed past Malone. "But don't
shoot him." She grabbed one officer's blue-clad arm. "My brother's
not armed, and he didn't do anything. Please don't shoot him." Her
voice broke on the last word.

Malone led her back to the couch. "We have no intention of
shooting your brother." He turned back to the two policemen. "You
can go."

They opened the door to leave, and that's when things got even
more crazy.

Several men in dark suits pushed through the doorway past the
two officers.

Wait a minute. I knew these guys. It was the G-men from our trip
to Huntington Beach. I felt my cheeks get warm as I remembered how
I'd been dressed the last time they'd seen me. Suddenly, my yoga pants
and sweatshirt seemed like a great fashion choice.

This time Agent I'm-Too-Serious-For-Myself Milner wasn't
focused on anyone else in the room. He was completely one hundred
and twenty percent focused on Detective Malone.

"What part of 'this is a federal case' did you not understand,
Detective?" No "hello", no "hey, what's happening." He went for the
jugular.

"Hello, Agent Milner." Malone went quiet. Always a bad sign. I
knew this from experience. "Maybe we could talk outside."

Agent Milner's stance said he was still on alert, but he seemed to
become aware of the tension in the room. He scanned the crowd. His
eyes lighted on Verdi and me, still parked on the couch.

I could see the moment recognition dawned.

"Oh, hell." He stood down. "All right, come on, Detective, let's
talk."

The two stepped outside, and, while we couldn't hear the heated
conversation, I got the general picture. Milner was not happy with

Malone. Malone was no happier with the way the evening had gone than I was.

I'd tried to help by having Verdi call Malone, but had only made things worse by giving Eugene the opportunity to get away.

I know you can't tell if a person is a murderer from talking with them. If you could, police departments around the nation would be able to cut down their case loads, there'd be no need for fancy forensics and we'd all be a lot safer. But even knowing it wasn't that simple, I'd been convinced that Eugene wasn't a risk. After talking to him, I was still convinced that he'd only run because he'd been scared.

He'd been misjudged before. The system had not been his friend, and he was afraid of a repeat performance.

Malone and Agent Milner came back inside. Agent Milner sat down in the chair across from Verdi. The same chair Eugene had occupied earlier.

"Is there anything you didn't tell Detective Malone?" he asked. "Anything at all?"

"No." Verdi whispered. "Nothing."

"All right." Milner ran his palm over his face. He looked rumpled, like he'd been at it all day and all night, without time for niceties like a fresh shirt or a change of clothes. "Young lady, if you hear from your brother, you are to call me directly." He handed Verdi a business card. "Do you understand?"

She nodded.

"And you," Agent Milner turned his attention to me. "*You*, Ms. Lamont, are to stay out of this business entirely." He paused. "Do you understand?"

Any shrinking violet would have wilted under the hard stare he leveled at me. But I'm from Texas, and we're made of sterner stuff.

I moved forward on the couch, level with him, so I was sure he could see the determination in my eyes.

"What I understand, Agent Milner, is that you think you can bully this poor girl who was trying to do the right thing by calling the police." I glared at Malone and came back to Agent Milner. "I understand you also think you can bully me, who is involved in this business whether I want to be or not. And"—I paused for effect—"I understand you have taken property that belongs to me. Property I expect to be returned immediately."

"What? What property?" He looked to Malone, who stood by the door. And who didn't seem at all inclined to jump in and help him. I imagined Malone had also been told to mind his own business.

"A family heirloom which was taken as evidence by the crime scene people and which has now been transferred to you. It's a brooch I was wearing when the stabbing victim fell against me, but it has nothing at all to do with your case. And I want it back. Pronto."

"Oh, hell." Agent Milner ran a hand through his salt-and-pepper hair. "A brooch?"

"Yes."

"Why me?" He glanced around at the room of people and then dropped his head and looked at the floor.

I couldn't answer his question, but I felt sure he'd gotten my point.

"All right, Ms. Lamont." He raised his head and looked at me. "I'll see what I can do to locate the whereabouts of this brooch."

"Great." I smiled my best Miss Congeniality smile. "Then we're on the same page, sugar." I reached over and patted his forearm.

Agent Milner stood. "And it would be great if you'd stay out of my investigation."

I bristled.

"Wait." He held up his hand in a stop gesture. "Before you get all over my case again."

"Okay." I stood also.

I was kind of wishing for my Tomb Raider outfit at this point. It was harder to be fierce in yoga pants and a sweatshirt.

"If you happen upon any information about the case in your daily work"—he pulled a card from his jacket—"you should call me. Directly."

I took the card from him and tucked it in my pocket. I didn't know if the fact I believed Blanche had lied about knowing the dead guy counted as information about the case. In truth, I didn't know for sure she'd lied. A more in-depth conversation with Blanche was definitely in order. Then I'd decide about calling Mr. FBI.

Agent Milner crossed to the door and motioned to his posse to join him. As he passed Malone, I heard him mutter, "Is she always such a pain in the butt?"

Malone made eye contact with me from across the room.

"You have no idea," he answered. "You have no idea."

Chapter Fifteen

THE NEXT MORNING, before I'd even showered, I called Blanche LeRue.

She answered on the first ring.

"Blanche, this is Caro Lamont."

"Do you have information from the Greys Matter donors?" The brisk and efficient Blanche was back. I'd be willing to bet she'd showered hours ago.

"No, I'm afraid this is about the murder investigation." I didn't see any reason to dance around the reason for my call. "Eugene, the missing waiter, showed up last night."

"He did?" I could picture her pacing as she talked.

"Yes, but then he disappeared again. The police came to question him, and then the FBI, but he was gone."

"The FBI?" There was a sharp intake of breath and then she went very quiet.

"That's mainly why I'm calling. The agent in charge asked that I let him know anything I find out about the man who was stabbed."

"Yes?" Her voice was still.

"And I believe you knew him before the night of the fund-raiser, and for some reason you're not admitting you did."

Absolute silence from the other end.

"Blanche?"

"Yes."

"If that's true, hon, it would be best if you talked to the FBI." I wished I could see her. It was difficult to gauge her reaction over the phone. "I don't know what exactly they're investigating, but it's not just a homicide. They've booted Laguna Beach PD off the case, so it's got to be something more."

"It's not that black and white, Caro. It's complicated." I could hear tapping. Probably her on her tablet computer. "I understand the awkward position this has put you in. Please continue to check in with my Greyhound owners. And please don't say anything about Dirk until we've had a chance to talk again."

"Agreed. But we need to talk soon." I couldn't let this go on for too long without contacting Agent Milner like I'd promised.

"Tomorrow," she said. "Ten o'clock at the Koffee Klatch."

"I'll be there."

I'd been pretty darned certain about Blanche hiding the fact she'd known Victor—or rather, Dirk—but her using his name confirmed it. I couldn't imagine what would make her keep such important information to herself. Good grief, a man was dead. She had to have a good reason. At least, I hoped it was a good reason.

Feeling relief at having handled the hardest task of the day, I showered, dressed, and reviewed my schedule. The sun was shining, the coffee was ready, and I was off to tackle the morning.

I'd thrown on my Vince khaki cargo pants, tank top, and a vintage black Chanel jacket that had been Diana's. Practical but fun. Sort of grunge meets old Hollywood. I liked it. My mama would not have approved.

I glanced next door as I backed out of the garage. I'd offered Verdi the option of staying with me last night. She'd declined, preferring to go back to her apartment. I knew she thought her brother might try to contact her there, but I also knew the FBI probably had both her place and the house next door under surveillance. Poor thing. She was really caught up in this mess now.

First on the list for today was Sam's grandmother and her Greyhounds.

Dmitri and Dorothea Drakos had raised Sam after his mother and stepfather had been killed in a car accident. His grandparents had dealt in olives, his stepfather had dealt in movies, and his birth father wasn't in the picture at all.

Dmitri had been gone for years, and his grandmother ran the business. According to Sam, she always really had, but had kept a low profile because it hadn't been an acceptable role for women when his grandparents had first started the olive business.

Her home was located in an area accessed off Laguna Canyon Road and sat on several acres of land. There was no guard to check in with, but there was an intercom for the gate, and, after I provided my name, the gates slid silently open.

As I drove up the long drive and parked in front of the multi-car garage, I felt my chest tighten. The terrain was different, but there was a feel about the place that reminded me of home, of the Montgomery ranch. I didn't dwell on it often, but there were times when a longing for the wide-open spaces where I'd grown up welled up inside me.

I got out of the car and grabbed my bag with the notes Verdi had compiled. Dorothea had two Italian Greyhounds, Ari and Angel. I rang the bell, and the door immediately opened to an extremely disheveled Sam.

His dark hair was mussed, his jeans were crumpled, and his knit shirt, while probably some designer label, looked like he'd been rolling around on the ground in it.

"Caro!" He flashed a heart-melting smile and kissed my cheek. "I'm so happy you are here. Come, Yia Yia is expecting you."

I followed. I knew very little Greek, but I knew *yia yia* (which he pronounced ya-ya) meant grandmother.

The house was one of those where the exterior was deceiving. Not that it looked small from the outside, but what you saw when you first walked up in no way prepared you for how big the home was inside. A bit different from the home I'd grown up in where everything was a bit in-your-face. If the decorating reflected the personality, I guess that'd be right, because Mama was of the if-you've-got-it-flaunt-it mind-set. The Drakos home was very elegant, but with an old-world flavor. Classic lines, rich warm colors, vibrant art on the walls. Family pictures lined the mantel, drapes were open to the outdoors, dog toys left a trail through the room. Elegant but lived-in.

"She's outside in the garden." Sam motioned for me to follow. "She'd live out there if she could."

He opened a wide patio door, and we walked onto a flagstone path which led to a courtyard lush with trees and foliage. Dorothea was cutting a couple of long-stemmed Bird of Paradise flowers. She dropped them into a vase of water on the nearby table and removed her gloves.

She was beautiful. Her hair and eyes were dark like Sam's, but where he was tall and athletic, she was small and round. "Carolina, I'm so glad to meet you properly at last." She took my hands in hers.

Though the touch was gentle, I sensed a powerful might lived inside that little body.

"So very nice to meet you, as well." I felt like I should curtsy. It was a bit like meeting a little Greek version of Queen Elizabeth.

"Did I not tell you, Yia Yia, how beautiful she is?"

"Yes, yes, Samuel. You might have mentioned it." She winked at me. "The fiery red hair, the porcelain skin, but in the warm eyes I see more. The beauty on the inside."

I felt my cheeks warm. "You're too kind."

"Come." She pointed with a small but sturdy hand to the table where she'd put the flowers. "I have a little *kolatsio* for us."

I looked at Sam.

"A snack," he explained. "I know you're here about the dogs, but I couldn't stop her."

"You." She pointed at him. "Go make yourself presentable."

"Be right back." Sam jogged back toward the house. "I'll wash up."

"He rolls around on the ground with the dogs." She indicated the two sleeping Greyhounds who lay in the shade of a large eucalyptus tree. "Come, let us sit."

She moved the vase of flowers to the middle and removed linens from plates of food. A small feast had been laid out on the table. Cheeses, some pastry triangles, and, of course, olives. There was also coffee and tea.

We sat and soon Sam joined us. "Presentable?" He patted his grandmother's arm and helped himself to a sliver of cheese.

Though he didn't live with his grandmother, Sam was clearly comfortable with her, and it was apparent he spent time in her company.

My mind slipped to all the times I'd enjoyed in my grandmother's big country kitchen or on the wide front porch at the ranch. She'd been a pillar in my life, and I missed her every day. In all honesty, the battle between Mel and me over Grandma Tillie's brooch really came down to the fact that my cousin and I both missed her like crazy. If we could agree on our mutual heartache, maybe we could sort things out. Maybe.

I shook myself from my musings, though the courtyard would have been an ideal place to sit and ponder, and returned to the conversation at hand.

"Your Greyhounds are beautiful," I accepted the cup of coffee Sam handed me. "Have you seen any changes in Ari and Angel since the ill-fated Greyhound event?"

"None at all." She dropped her hand to her side, and the two dogs came and nuzzled it. "This is Ari." She patted the black dog. "And this is Angel." She scratched under the dappled dog's chin. "I only agreed to the visit as a thinly-veiled ploy to get a chance to meet you."

The dogs worked their way under the table, and one leaned against her legs and the other against Sam. A very loyal and affectionate breed, these two Greyhounds were no exception. Moving fast or cuddle bugs.

"I got the dogs very young. Neither had raced, but were born to a racing mother and an unknown father. Often, those dogs are destroyed by the breeder because the lineage isn't clear and they can't race them." She reached over and patted Ari, who'd now wormed his way onto Sam's lap.

"That's awful." I couldn't imagine.

"This breeder had a heart, though, and turned the litter over to Greys Matter, and I was blessed to have these two come live with me."

I wasn't aware of the practice, but it certainly explained Blanche LeRue's passion for the cause even more. And also explained why Dorothea had talked Sam into serving on the board of Greys Matter.

"Blanche seems concerned the incident at the fund-raiser and all of the news around the unsolved murder may hurt the rescue's efforts." I looked to Sam. "Have you seen any indication of those kinds of problems?"

"Nothing so far." He leaned back in his chair, one tanned arm thrown over the back, the other resting on the dog in his lap. Even scruffy, he looked like he'd walked off a *GQ* photo shoot—handsome, casual, comfortable with himself. And he seemed totally unaware how gorgeous he was. "What do you hear on the investigation?"

I gave him a brief summary. I left out the part where Verdi and I were dressed like video game chicks and almost arrested by the FBI. It didn't seem appropriate in front of his *yia yia*. I ended with an account of Eugene's appearance and subsequent disappearance last night.

"There's been nothing in the news," he said. "I had no idea."

"Well, I don't mean to snoop." I popped an olive in my mouth.

Sam's raised brow said he was not buying my disclaimer.

"But is the rescue okay financially?" I asked. "Blanche seemed worried."

"Nothing I've seen in the financial reports would indicate any problems. The fund-raising event was to be the biggest infusion of cash, but overall, the donations meet the expenses." Sam rubbed his jaw. "But I could take a closer look if you think there's a concern."

I shook my head. "Blanche is very competent. I don't think there's a need. I'm meeting with her tomorrow anyway."

"Our Samuel, he's very good at financial things." Dorothea nibbled at one of the cheese pastries. "It's important the donor's contributions are given the proper care."

"I agree completely." From what I'd heard it wasn't just Sam. Yia Yia Dorothea herself was a bit of a financial expert. "I hope to know more after I talk with Blanche."

"Good." She nodded.

"I had better get going." I stood. "I've got another appointment coming up, and it's my day to volunteer at the ARL. Thank you so much for your hospitality."

Sam removed Angel from his lap and got up, too. "I'll walk you out."

Ari scrambled to his feet, and both dogs looked at Sam, eyes hopeful, ears at attention, sleek bodies ready to run.

"Ah, you want to play some more, don't you?"

Sam's grandmother also stood, took my hands, and gave them a squeeze. "Come back again. Soon." Her look was just as expectant as the two Greyhounds.

Sam walked me back through the house and out to my car. I slid in, and he shut the door and then leaned in for a swift kiss. "You're a hit with Yia Yia Dot, Caro *kopelia mou.*" He touched my cheek with his knuckle. "Not easy to do. She's a tough cookie."

I knew all about tough cookies. I came from a long line of tough cookies. But I was glad I'd passed muster with Yia Yia Dot.

"She's a gem, Sam. Please thank her again for the snacks, even though I now need to add at least a mile to my evening run."

I started the car and put it in gear. "I'll call you tomorrow after I've talked to Blanche."

Chapter Sixteen

AS THE AFTERNOON went on, my confidence waned.

Should I have agreed to meet Blanche before talking to the FBI? By the time I finished my appointments, done my stint at the Laguna Beach Animal Rescue League, arrived home for the day, and Dogbert and I had circled the block, I'd had several internal conversations with myself about my plan to meet Blanche LeRue.

Blanche sure as heck wasn't dangerous. But she had outright lied about knowing the dead guy. And we were meeting in a public place.

In the end, I convinced myself "better safe than sorry." I know, y'all are surprised at that conclusion. But, fresh in my mind was my misjudgment of Eugene. I'd had him and then had just sent him off to change out of his droid jammies. I had no thought he'd escape. I try to do the right thing, I really do.

As soon as I had all the animals fed, I called the number Agent Milner had given me.

FBI Agent Milner called me back within fifteen minutes.

"You have some information?" Mr. No-Time-for-Pleasantries asked.

"Here's the thing, hon." I could picture his impatience, but I forged on. "I'm not sure if I do or if I don't, so let me run this by you."

"All right."

"I talked to Blanche LeRue, the Greyhound rescue's executive director, and I mentioned that one of the Greyhound owners had reported seeing Victor, the dead guy, at the rescue office."

"Uh-huh."

"When I mentioned it to Blanche, she denied having ever met the guy prior to the event where he was killed. But she acted kinda funny about it."

"So you want me to talk to Ms. LeRue?"

"No. I, um, called her after you stopped by next door the other night, and I suggested she talk to you, but she wanted to meet with me first to explain. So we're meeting tomorrow morning at a local coffee shop. I think it would be good if you'd join us."

"I could do that."

"Agent Milner?"

"Yes."

"It would probably be best if you could look like a regular person tomorrow. You know, not look like you work for the FBI?" Looking like he usually did, it would be obvious to everyone in the vicinity that he was some sort of law enforcement.

"What kind of disguise would you like me to wear? My X-Men outfit?" There was a slight snicker from the other end.

"Very funny." I kind of regretted my effort to be helpful at that point. "Perhaps a pair of shorts and a golf shirt, if you own any."

"Believe me, Ms. Lamont, you don't want to see these legs, but I'll see what I can do to disguise myself as a native. Where is this coffee shop?"

"It's the Koffee Klatch right on PCH." I gave him the address. "We're meeting at ten o'clock."

"I'll be there." And with a click, he was gone.

THE NEXT MORNING, I arrived early at the Koffee Klatch, ready for my usual. Verdi was in place behind the counter and had my latte ordered before I had the words out of my mouth.

I picked up my drink and pastry at the counter and looked for a table. Outdoors would be best because Blanche could easily spot me, and also it was less likely we'd be overheard. I found an open table and set my cup and plate down.

Within minutes, Agent Milner arrived.

He'd done a good job. Navy chinos, a sky blue striped polo shirt, and a lightweight tan windbreaker to cover his sidearm. I'd learned from being around Detective Malone and his crew (don't ask) that you hardly ever see plainclothes law-enforcement without a jacket or vest of some kind.

I didn't really think Blanche was dangerous, but I was somehow comforted by the fact that Agent Milner was present.

"Ms. Lamont." He tipped his ball cap and sat down at the table. "You look nice today."

I was taken aback.

"Why, that's sweet of you to say. I don't have any pet appointments this morning, and I'm having lunch with my friend, Diana." I glanced down at the turquoise-and-white Diane von Furstenberg sundress I'd pulled from my closet that morning. Unremarkable, but a whole lot different from how I'd been dressed each of the times he'd seen me before.

No wonder the man treated me like I was a couple of sandwiches shy of a picnic.

"By your friend, Diana, you mean Diana Knight?" Agent Milner took a sip of his coffee.

"Yes, we've been friends since I moved here." Not much got a reaction from Agent Milner, but I could see from his face he was a little star-struck. Most people are by Diana, and then they're equally shocked she is so down to earth.

"Diana's an avid supporter of animal causes, so we've worked together on several events." I explained.

"You're not a native Californian?" I was impressed at Agent Milner's effort at small talk.

"What gave me away?" I laughed. "You're right. I'm from the great state of Texas."

"You haven't always worked with problem pets?" he continued.

"No, my education is in counseling psychology." I turned the coffee cup on its saucer. "People counseling." I added.

"And what brought you to California?"

"A new start. After—" I started to explain, but stopped myself. Something about the expression on Agent Milner's face told me he already knew all the details of my background.

I'd almost forgotten who I was talking to. Of course, the FBI had run background checks on Verdi and on me after the incident at Kyle's house. And all my Texas mess would've shown up. My ex-husband's involvement with a patient, the loss of both of our licenses to practice, the lies, the divorce, the media frenzy.

"Go on."

"I think you already know all about me and why I left Texas."

"Perhaps," he said, his eyes steady and his voice low, "but I'd rather hear your version."

"Not important." I set my cup down on the table. "Not why we're here."

We were done talking about me. I'd had enough invasion of privacy to last a lifetime. My ex-husband had made sure of that, and I'd come to southern California to escape the notoriety. That, and to escape my overbearing mother.

Definitely, I was done.

Until Blanche got here, Agent John Milner and I could talk about the weather.

Chapter Seventeen

THE PERENNIALLY-prompt Blanche had not shown up by ten-fifteen.

By ten-thirty, Agent Milner was beyond his legal limit as far as patience, and I'd polished off my scone and sugar-free hazelnut latte. I know, I know. It doesn't do much good to hold the calories on the coffee drink and load them up on the pastry. I like to think they somehow cancel each other out.

Milner had finished off his coffee also. He was a black coffee kind of guy, no froufrou coffee drinks for Mr. FBI.

"She apparently changed her mind." He pushed his ball cap back and squinted into the sun.

"I guess so." Either that, or she really was the killer and had seen I'd brought reinforcements.

Oh, man. Ax that idea. I'd officially lost my mind. Even if Blanche were the killer, broad daylight at the Koffee Klatch was not the best pick for doing me in.

Agent Milner and I were fixing to bail when Alana Benda walked past, her Italian Greyhounds on a leash.

She wore Rogiani custom-fit three-quarter leggings and a spandex halter top from their Rebel collection. High-stakes fitness wear.

Toned and muscular, she strode into the coffee shop. Long spray-tanned legs glided through the busy coffee shop, her highlighted blond strands strategically flipped over one shoulder, and five-hundred-dollar sunglasses perched on her perfect nose.

Milner stared, mesmerized, totally slack-jawed, and lost in some fantasy world. His head followed her movements like Dogbert follows my path to get his treats from the pantry at home.

She was only inside a short time and then came out with her smoothie. She noticed me and came toward our table, Louie and Lexie beside her.

I leaned over and whispered to the speechless FBI agent, "Close your mouth, sugar, you're gonna get drool on your nice shirt."

"Hello, Caro." Alana's two dogs had matching T-shirts, aka tummy warmers, in a similar fabric to her workout clothes.

Now, don't get me wrong, I'm not against clothing for animals. Especially animals like Greyhounds who can sometimes get chilled in places with air conditioning.

"Hi, Alana." I reached down and stroked the dogs who nuzzled my hand. "Meet my friend, John."

"Nice to meet you." She held out a hand weighed down by diamonds. The tennis bracelet sparkled against her tanned wrist, and a humongous diamond solitaire graced her ring finger.

I was afraid Agent Milner was going to kiss it.

"No doggie clients this morning?" Alana shifted the leash and pushed her sunglasses up to look at me.

"I was supposed to meet Blanche LeRue here, but she's late."

"That's not like Blanche."

"No, it's not." I agreed. "We had some things to discuss."

"What kind of things?" Alana's artificially aqua eyes shot to Agent Milner and back to me.

So much for thinking Agent Milner could blend in.

"About the rescue group." I was purposely vague in my answer. The woman who was hardly ever interested in anyone but herself seemed a little too interested in what I planned to talk to Blanche about.

"Oh." Her lips formed a perfect circle. I could practically see the wheels turning in her brain. "Nice to meet you." She nodded to Agent Milner and slid her sunglasses back on. "Got to get going. We've got yoga class this morning." She picked up her drink, and she and her Greys glided away.

Agent Milner watched her go until she was completely out of sight. "The dogs do an exercise class?"

"There's a 'Doggie and Me' yoga class." I explained.

Milner looked blank.

"Kind of like the 'Mommy and Me' classes they do for babies."

"Babies do yoga?"

I laughed at his dumbfounded look. "You've got to get out more, hon."

He shook his head like a dog shaking water from its fur. "I'm busy chasing bad guys, and people are taking their dogs to exercise classes."

"Some people." I grinned.

Agent Milner and I parted ways, and I headed to my office. I'd promised to let him know if I heard from Blanche, but I'd already tried to reach her and gotten no answer.

Whatever she'd been nervous about sharing regarding what she knew about the man who'd been killed, she must have decided to keep to herself. If that were the case, there wasn't much I could do about it.

When I arrived, Dave's office door was open, so I took the opportunity to stop by. Though we'd been in the same suite for several years, it wasn't like we saw each other that much. I couldn't think of the last time I'd been inside his office. To tell you the truth, I didn't even know for sure when he'd married Alana. It seemed to my recollection he hadn't been married when we'd first met which would have been when I rented my office space. He was clearly crazy about his wife, and she was crazy about his money.

His desk was stacked with files and papers. He'd hung his suit jacket on a hall tree in the corner and was working in shirt sleeves, but still managed to have a neat buttoned-down look about him.

"I just saw Alana and the dogs." I said.

He continued to work head down.

"At the Koffee Klatch."

He looked up from his paperwork, startled, like he'd just realized I'd been talking to him. "What was that?"

"I said I saw your wife at the Koffee Klatch. She was on her way to yoga." I leaned against his doorway.

"Oh, yeah. It's always some class." Distracted, he looked back down at the spreadsheet on his desk. "This afternoon, it's the exclusive 'royal treatment' at The Spa. Difficult to get an appointment. Probably costs as much as if they're hosting a royal."

Oh, my. Was that sarcasm I detected?

"I was supposed to meet Blanche LeRue," I explained. "But she was a no-show."

"What?" He looked up again, his light blue eyes suddenly focused instead of distracted, and I wondered why. Had Blanche perhaps confided in Dave?

"I tried her cell phone and the number at the Greys Matter office, but didn't get an answer."

"Why were you meeting Blanche?"

"Oh, you know, she had asked me to check in with the Greyhound owners who had dogs at the fund-raiser."

"She called you or you called her?' he asked.

"I called her." I wasn't sure why it mattered.

"And you were meeting to talk about the dogs?"

"That's right."

"She isn't at the office?"

"I didn't drive by, but no one answered the phone."

He sure had a lot of questions when just a few minutes ago he'd been trying to get rid of me.

I picked up my messages and my files for the rest of the afternoon and headed back to my car. Days like this, I wondered why I even kept an office. The trusty Mercedes often ended up being where I spent more time.

DIANA AND I HAD decided on La Mie for lunch. That decision meant we'd probably let ourselves be talked into dessert.

It went without saying, between the earlier scone and now this lunch, I would have to take Dogbert for a very long walk later to make up for the calories. But Dog never minded a longer walk time, and La Mic's desserts were always worth it.

Diana was already there when I arrived, and the waiter stopped by within minutes. We gave our orders, and he whisked the menus away, replacing them with a basket of fresh herbed bread.

"So." Diana leaned in. "What's new in the murder investigation?"

I filled her in on Eugene's appearance and disappearance. Also, my discovery that Blanche had lied about not knowing the dead man.

"Oh, dear." Diana sipped her Perrier. "I'm sure if Blanche claimed she didn't know the man, she must have had a very good reason. She's a good egg."

"You know her better than I do, hon." I trusted Diana's judgment, but I knew there were secrets being kept, and until those involved started telling the truth, there was no chance of unraveling what had really happened.

"Blanche doesn't have any family." Diana brushed a crumb from the table. "The Greyhounds and their cause have been her family. I'm sure she would never do anything to endanger the rescue."

Diana's defense certainly rang true. Everything Blanche had said to me supported the impression that the Greyhound rescue effort was her life's work. I didn't think she'd do anything to put the organization at risk. But the question remained, would Blanche do something awful to protect it?

"She'd agreed to meet me this morning to talk about it, but didn't show up." I took a sip of water. "I feel bad about not talking to her first, but I had to share the info with the FBI guy."

"Of course." Diana patted my hand. "Would you like me to call her? I've gotten to know her fairly well, what with being on the board."

"It couldn't hurt. What's the board's reaction to what's happened?" I asked.

The waiter appeared with our salads. The restaurant's sesame-crusted ahi salad was legendary, and today's did not disappoint.

Diana picked up her fork. "They'd like whoever killed this man to be found."

"Is the rescue group in any financial trouble?" I felt I had to ask. "Blanche acted concerned about losing donors, but when I talked to Sam, he seemed to think the group's finances were in good shape."

"I agree with Sam. On the last financial report we got, everything looked good." She took a bite. "Dave Benda is our accountant, and he's always given a very thorough report."

"That's a relief. Maybe Blanche is just hyper-sensitive to losing supporters when she's worked so hard to create a good organization."

"What about this young man, Eugene?"

"The FBI is still looking for him. I feel terrible for Verdi. She believes he's not involved, and, honestly, I do too. I think he's terrified of going back to prison, and he doesn't trust the system."

"It would look better for him if he'd turn himself in."

"I know. But he's apparently gone into hiding again."

We finished our salads, and, without too much convincing on the part of our waiter, we agreed to share a La Mie specialty, their decadent chocolate and caramel sundae topped with toasted pecans.

"We're bad." I said to Diana.

"We are," she agreed. "And that's one of our better qualities."

Once we were finished, I knew it would take more than one long walk with Dogbert to burn off the calories I'd just consumed.

"Don't forget we have our self-defense class tonight." Diana reminded me. "I'm sure Betty will keep us entertained."

"That's right." I smiled, thinking of the woman and her bizarre eyebrows. "So far it's been better than I thought it would be."

Diana leaned closer. "Isn't that our instructor, Matt, across the way with Alana Benda?"

Diana tipped her blond head in their direction so as not to be obvious, and I followed the angle.

It was Matt and Alana. Head to head, oblivious to the other restaurant patrons.

He was more dressed up than I'd ever seen him. She'd changed out of her yoga clothes, and, though I didn't know the designer, I was pretty sure the hot red backless flounce dress had been designed for a body such as Alana's. A body that was *not* getting the exclusive "royal treatment" because she was not at The Spa where her husband thought she was.

The waiter brought our check, and, after we paid, I walked Diana to her car. I filled her in on my conversation with Dave Benda earlier and his mention of Alana's appointment at The Spa, plus his unnatural interest in my meeting with Blanche.

"I can't imagine Blanche wouldn't call you if she couldn't make it." Diana shook her head. "That's not like her."

Almost the same words Blanche had used the day I'd been at her house. She'd been through a lot lately and had seemed more together, but still scattered, when I'd stopped by the office. Maybe the poor woman had simply spaced it off.

Diana promised to give Blanche a call as soon as she got home and let me know tonight at our "Be Safe" class what she was able to find out.

"See you there," I called as I walked away.

Tonight, I wanted to be sure to ask Matt, our instructor, how Chachi, his Maltese, was doing at the dog park. And if I could work seeing him and Alana Benda at La Mie into the conversation, I'd be able to gauge his reaction.

Also, less importantly, I also needed to remember to dress more appropriately for this week's class. Last week, my eighty-year-old friend had been more with it than me.

Maybe this thirty-year-old was the one who needed to get out more.

Chapter Eighteen

THIS TIME, I WAS properly dressed for the "Be Safe" self-defense class.

High-end pink Phillip Lim track pants, and an equally fashionable tank top, both from Neiman Marcus. Mama Kat would have approved.

Although I don't think Kat Lamont, née Montgomery, had ever in her life gone out in public in exercise clothes. She was of the ladies-don't-sweat school of upbringing.

I'd been reminded for years: *Horses sweat, men perspire, and ladies glow.*

And if a lady were to "glow," she would need to do it in the privacy of her own home or in a sauna at one of those exclusive spas like the one Alana had been supposed to be visiting. Yep, it was good I was hundreds of miles away from those expectations.

I looked around the fitness studio. Matt was at the front of the room talking to one of the attendees. I spotted Diana near the back of the room. She was chatting with Betty Foxx.

I had to admit, I'd kind of looked forward to seeing the funny and feisty Betty again. But I'd have to wait until Betty wasn't around to ask if Diana had been successful in reaching Blanche. I didn't need Betty reporting back to Mel, and Mel making another phone call that would get Mama Kat riled up.

I joined them.

"Hello again, hon." I gave Diana's shoulders a squeeze. She looked classy, as always. Perfect but subtle makeup, blond hair styled and sprayed in place. Tonight, her workout clothes matched her bright blue eyes.

"Hello, sweetie. My, don't you look gorgeous." She smiled. "If you weren't my friend, I'd hate you."

I turned to the tiny woman beside her. "Hello, Betty, good to see you."

Tonight, she'd gone for a nice pale lavender look. Paisley silk pajamas. Same pearls. Same bright white sneakers. Same black, patent leather pocketbook held close. This time, she wore purple "paw-lish" on her fingernails.

"Hello, Carmen." Her gray eyes narrowed as she looked me over. Clearly, I was not to be trusted. Guess she'd been talking to my cousin, Mel.

This time, it appeared Betty had actually used an eye makeup product on her brows. They were nicely drawn with little feathery strokes. The problem was, they were blue. It was hard to look away.

"Okay, let's get started." Matt's booming voice drew everyone's attention. "Most self-defense classes teach you what to do as long as your assailant does what's expected. Problem is, nine times out of ten, they don't. What we're going to show you is how to use a few easy techniques and the element of surprise to protect yourself in the most common types of attacks. For the first part of the class, we'll talk about what you can do if someone physically attacks. The second part of the class, we'll talk about what if your attacker has a weapon."

"Hubba hubba." Betty pointed a purple-tipped finger toward the front of the room.

Two big beefy guys had joined the class. "Zeke and Erik will be helping out tonight."

I glanced over at Diana. "Oh, I agree." Her blue eyes twinkled. "Hubba hubba, indeed."

Matt moved to the center of the room. "Let's split you into two smaller groups so we can practice." We obediently formed two groups and Matt assigned a "hubba hubba" guy to each one.

"Here are the important things to keep in mind." Matt stood between the two clusters of women. "Move fast without telegraphing what you're going to do. If your attacker has a grip on you, use the strongest parts of your body to break free.

"If he comes from behind, like this," Matt demonstrated. "Then stomp on his foot, kick him in the shins, or an elbow to the ribs is always effective."

He kept a careful distance from Lavender Betty who mimicked each move as he talked about it. Her silk pajamas flew like a lavender veil dance as she quickly adopted each move.

"If he's got your arm, like this"—Matt grabbed the arm of the woman standing closest to him—"use all your strength to break that hold, moving in the direction of his thumb."

"Here," Betty said to one of the burly young men. "Grab my arm."

He did and she immediately pulled back on his thumb. He winced, but to his credit, didn't cry out.

"If he doesn't have a hold of you, don't let him. Try to avoid moves that will allow him to grab you. For instance, kick him in the shin or knee."

Betty backed up and lifted her white tennis shoe as if to strike, but the young bodybuilder backed away out of reach.

"That allows you to keep your balance," Matt went on. "If you go for the groin, although it will cause more pain for him, it could leave you vulnerable. You could fall. He could grab your leg.

"If you have an object like a backpack, purse or umbrella, hit him hard and decisively with it."

Betty swung her black patent-leather purse with enough force that she continued for two full twirls. Luckily, no one was in range.

"Okay, ladies, let's practice." Matt motioned to the two other guys to assist.

Betty had her hand up, but Matt was not about to call on her. "Mike," she called. "Mike?"

"It's Matt." He walked over to her. "Yes, Betty."

"Right." Betty opened her handbag and pulled out a canister of pepper spray. "Wouldn't it just be easier to douse 'em with this."

She had her finger on the trigger and pointed at Matt's face. He quickly plucked the canister from her fingers. "Let's put this away, shall we?"

He dropped it back into her open bag.

"It's effective, but you may not have time to get something like that out of your bag." Matt walked back to the front.

Zeke, who was assigned to our group, went through each of the moves with us and, like Matt, emphasized that we should use our individual strengths to get away from an assailant. I was tall and could probably elbow someone in the ribs. Diana was more petite and might want to go for a kick to the knee.

We took a short break before the next session, and I took the opportunity to ask Betty about any Greyhound clients who shopped at Bow Wow.

"You investigating that murder?" Betty asked. "Cookie said you would be."

"Not really. I'm more concerned with the dogs."

"Yeah, right." Betty sniffed. "That Detective Malone is hot."

"It's a federal case now," I explained. "Malone is no longer involved."

"So the feds have Cookie's brooch?" she asked.

"I didn't say that." I didn't need her running to tell Mel I'd lost possession of Grandma Tillie's brooch to federal evidence.

"Some of those Greyhound people shop at Bow Wow," Betty noted. "Those are nice dogs."

I wondered if Betty knew any of the people from the rescue group. Marjory and Raymond Whedon had had some high-end toys for their dogs. Alana had probably purchased her dog's jackets from Mel's shop. Bow Wow carried a line of clothing specifically for the breed.

"You have people you see that need those kind of things, you should send them to Bow Wow Boutique. After all, you two are family whether you're talking to each other or not."

Diana stayed silent, clearly getting a kick out of my lecture from the five-foot tall, blue-eyebrowed gnome.

"We have this customer, Lenny Santucci," Betty continued, on a roll. "He has this wiener dog, Pickles, who he says is depressed." She used her two "paw-lished" index fingers to make the corners of her mouth turn down into a sad face. "Cookie tells him he should call you. See? See how that works?"

"Uh-huh." I saw. It was nice of Mel to refer people to me, but I'd talked with Lenny before and wasn't sure we were on the same page as far as how to deal with a depressed dachshund.

It was good it was time to start the second half of the class.

In the next session the "hubba hubba" guys sat out while Matt talked to us about situations where our attacker might have a weapon such as a gun or a knife.

"Let's start with a gun. If your attacker is close to you"—Matt demonstrated with one of the female assistants from the first night— "you may have a chance to disarm them. The technique you'll learn and practice will show you how to distract them, move to the side, grab the muzzle, quickly slap the tender muscles of your attacker's forearm, and get away."

He pointed a fake gun at the girl's head. She screamed, moved to the side, grabbed the gun he still held, slapped his forearm, and took the gun.

It all happened so fast, it was like magic. I could see where someone who thought they had the upper hand would be surprised.

Zeke and Erik practiced with us, while Matt went from group to group making suggestions.

When it was Diana's turn, she surprised us all with a sharp high-pitched scream. Actually, that undersells it. It was, by far, the shrillest, most ear-splitting scream I've ever witnessed. And remember, I've lived through the Miss Texas pageant preliminaries where hormones run rampant.

"Hey, that's a good scream, lady." Betty looked at Diana with new respect. "How do you do that?"

"Method acting." Diana explained. "I used it in all those horror movies I was in, like *I Married a Zombie*. I did a lot of those early in my career. Just imagine you're confronted with the thing you're most frightened of, take a big deep breath, and let it rip."

We all had to try it, and soon the room was filled with twenty-some women screaming for their lives. Matt finally asked us to quit.

"Okay now, let's try the other part of the exercise." Matt looked like he'd need a belt of something more than a health shake once the evening was over.

He demonstrated again: the move to the side, grab the weapon, slap the attacker's forearm, and take the gun. We practiced the move over and over with the hard rubber guns, each of us taking a turn at disarming Zeke and Erik. It was great practice, but I was pretty it sure was much harder if the guy you were faced with held a real gun. One that could discharge at any moment.

Matt dismissed the class, but was quickly surrounded by women with questions about the use of the technique. None of us had gotten too excited about his cautions on jogging with a buddy or talking someone out of attacking us. But disarming a gunman, now that was exciting. I guessed I'd have to call him about Chachi. And about his relationship with Alana Benda.

As we walked to where we'd parked, Diana reported no luck in reaching Blanche. She'd try again in the morning and let me know.

Betty race-walked down the block and hopped into a little Mini Cooper. She started the car and pulled out, squealing her tires when she turned the corner. As she drove past, she waved a lavender-clad arm out the window.

I chuckled at the sight. I'd just bet Pajama Betty kept her boss on her toes.

It had been a long day, and it wasn't until I got home that I remembered I'd meant to stop by the office and pick up my files for the next day's appointments.

Chapter Nineteen

AFTER THE PAST few days of phony identities, half-truths, and blue eyebrows, I thought I was prepared for anything.

I wasn't.

I arrived at the office still amused by the thought of Betty giving Mel a hard time. I was ready for a full day of doing what I loved. Working with people who loved their pets, but who just needed a nudge and a little education to improve things for both. What could be better?

It was a light appointment day, but I still opted for clothes that could take it if I ended up on the floor rolling around with misbehaving pets. Blue jeans, white T-shirt, blue scarf and I was out the door.

I'd forgotten a hair band and couldn't immediately find one in my bag, so I left the top up on the convertible. My hair is uncontrollable enough in good conditions—in the wind, all bets were off. I didn't want to scare clients.

Verdi was at the reception desk. Dave's office was dark. I could see Kay, the real estate agent in the other office. She was on the phone animatedly closing a deal. Things were looking up in the housing market. Suzanne, the psychic, wasn't in. Her office was also lights out, but that wasn't unusual. She often came in at different times. Who knew? Perhaps the psychic vibes were better at certain times of day. And may I just say, how disappointed in her I am?

Where was the professional courtesy? If she had a pet with problems, I'd help her free and clear. If she needed real estate advice, Kay would advise. What in the Sam Hill was the use of having a psychic in your office group if she didn't see the bad juju coming your way and warn you?

I stopped at the desk. "Have you heard anything from Eugene?" I had to ask, though I was sure Verdi would have let me know if she had.

"No. Nothing." Verdi shook her burgundy locks. "I wish he

would call or text, and at least let me know he's okay."

I wished he would, too. If he had information about the man who was killed, he needed to talk to Malone or Agent Milner. The news media had gone silent on the case—no updates of any kind. So who knew if Eugene realized the FBI was now investigating?

"I'm sure he will when he thinks he can." I gave Verdi's hand a squeeze. The poor thing looked like she hadn't slept in days.

"I sure hope so."

"Thanks for your help with the spreadsheet of Greyhound owners. I think I'm almost through the list." I turned toward my office. "I'll be able to provide a report to Blanche as soon as I get my notes filled in."

I settled at my desk and began the task of transferring my handwritten notes to the spreadsheet. I figured I'd get them ready and then drop them off at the Greys Matter office sometime today.

I'd just gotten started when my cell phone rang.

I dug the phone from my purse. "Hello?"

It was Sam.

"Caro." His voice was quiet. "I need to tell you something before you hear it from someone else or on the television." Sam's voice was even and steady, but I sensed this wasn't going to be good news.

"Blanche LeRue is dead."

I felt cold to my core.

"What? How?" I could hardly get the words out.

"We've been told it was suicide. I don't have any other details." He waited for me to compose myself. "The police are contacting all the Greys Matter board members."

"Dave's not here."

"I imagine they called him, just as they called me."

"Diana?" I asked. Diana is so spunky, sometimes we all forget about her advanced age. This would be a shock—she was close to Blanche. Much closer than the rest of us.

"The police have agreed I can be the one to tell her. I am on my way to her house now."

Leave it to Sam to think about how best to break the news to Diana. "Sam, I don't know what to say. Or what to think."

"I know, *kopelia mou.*" His voice was soft. "I'm sure we'll know more soon. I just didn't want you to have the shock of someone else telling you. Or worse, hearing it on the news."

"Thanks, Sam. I appreciate it." I looked up to see Verdi standing in my doorway. "I'll talk to you later."

"Okay." I hit the disconnect button and sat staring at the wall.

"Caro?" Verdi said from beside me. "Are you all right?"

I turned to face her. "Blanche LeRue is dead."

"How?" She dropped into one of the side chairs. "What happened?"

"I'm not sure. Sam said the police are still sorting things out, but they think it was suicide."

"Oh, wow."

We sat for a while without speaking, each of us lost in our thoughts.

I hadn't asked any details about timing, but I had to wonder if Blanche had already been dead when I'd sat waiting for her at the Koffee Klatch.

I felt sick.

Verdi didn't know Blanche personally at all, but she had to know the search for her brother would intensify. Blanche's death might be a suicide, but the likelihood it was somehow linked to the other death was a pretty sure bet.

After a few minutes of sitting in silence, Verdi rose. "Is there anything I can get you?"

"No thanks, hon." I tried to collect myself. I looked down at the spreadsheet of Greyhound owners I'd been working on when Sam called. What had happened with Blanche? Suicide didn't make sense to me. There must be another explanation.

"Okay, let me know if there's anything I can help with." Verdi slipped out of my office and went back to her station at the front desk.

I sat for a while and tried to get my bearings before gathering my things to begin my appointments for the day.

AN HOUR LATER, I was in my car and headed to my first appointment of the day. I drove past the Greys Matter office on my way through town. There was a "Closed" sign in the window.

I needed to know more about what had happened, and there was really only one person who could fill in the blanks. I dialed Detective Malone's number and he picked up.

"Are you at Blanche's house?" I asked without preamble.

"I am, but don't even think about coming here, Caro." The tone of his voice was no-nonsense, and I'd bet the look on his handsome face was, too.

"So Blanche's death must be considered a homicide if you're there."

"No, it's pretty clearly a suicide." I could hear the bustle and buzz of conversation in the background. It sounded like a full crew.

"It can't be."

"Why do you think that?" Malone voice sharpened. "There was a note signed by Ms. LeRue."

Malone was being summoned; I could hear someone calling his name.

"So is this your case or the FBI's?" I asked quickly.

"Oh no, this one is ours."

"I may have information." Not strictly true. I didn't have much information; I mostly had a lot of questions.

"Stop by the office later this afternoon. I'll be in." He clicked off before I could say "no thanks" or "okay" or even good-bye.

My first appointment of the day was an easy one. It was a follow-up with a regular client, Ellen, who routinely took in foster animals. She had a new foster pup, and just wanted to make sure she was socializing him properly with her regular brood. Ramone was a little Pomeranian dog whose former owner had surrendered him at the ARL because he was too active. However, at Ellen's, he seemed to be doing fine with her other animals. I made a few suggestions, but her instincts were good, and Ellen had enough experience that she was already on the right track.

You'd be surprised at the number of people who adopted a dog in good faith and then, at the first sign of a problem, brought them back to the shelter. I'm sure they start out with good intentions, but rescues often need time to adjust. Which is especially true if the home already has pets. If adoptive families can understand what's going on, then they can make the changes needed to assimilate the new fur kid into the family. Too many people give up far too soon.

Okay, off my soapbox.

As I walked to my car, it occurred to me I hadn't asked about Blanche's dogs. Blaze and Trixie had to be lost without her. There was nothing I could do for Blanche at this point, but the one thing I could do was make sure her two Greyhounds were taken care of.

Her dogs were another reason that the idea Blanche LeRue had killed herself didn't fit. Even if she had, she would have made sure the dogs were taken care of first.

Maybe she had. Maybe they hadn't been at the house. In any case, I needed to find out what had happened with the dogs, or it would continue to bug me. I called Malone's cell, but the call went directly to voicemail. I tried the police station next.

Lorraine answered, and I explained to her I was concerned about Blanche LeRue's dogs and hadn't been able to reach Malone.

"He's still at the house, Caro," she reported. "I expect he'll be back in the station this afternoon, but he's been over there all morning."

"Thanks, Lorraine. I'm between appointments, so I might just drive by."

"Uh-huh." She didn't say not to, and I couldn't see her roll her eyes, but we both knew what kind of a reception I would get from Malone.

When I pulled the Mercedes up in front of the house, it appeared the crew was wrapping things up. Crime scene techs were packing up their gear. Detective Malone stood in the front yard talking on his cell phone.

One of the techs approached me. "Can I help you with something?"

"I'm a friend," I explained. "And I was concerned about Blanche's dogs."

"They're still in the house." He pointed to the house. "I'm not sure what the plan is for them. You'd have to talk to Malone."

"Thanks." I looked at the open front door and was tempted. There was no yellow crime scene tape stretched across the entry, and I was truly concerned about Blaze and Trixie. But Malone and I'd had a previous incident with an unmarked crime scene, and I was taking no chances. I would wait for him to finish his call.

I watched him pace as he talked on the phone. Tall, dark, and intense. All cop, all business. For some reason, I imagined it might be Agent Milner on the other end. I stayed in the shade by my car until he was done and then approached him.

"I thought I told you not to come here." He tucked his cell into the pocket of his jeans.

"You did. But I forgot to ask about the dogs, and then I couldn't reach you."

"They're still in the house. I called Don Furry at the ARL about what to do with them."

I smiled to myself. See, he could be trained. A year ago, Malone would have just had them dropped off at the pound.

"What did Don say?"

"He said normally they would have called Blanche in a situation like this."

That was true. Blanche was our go-to Greyhound person.

"Did Don have another suggestion?"

"He thought they'd be able to either accommodate them at the shelter or find a temporary foster home for them."

"I can drop them off," I offered.

"Great." No hesitation. Malone headed toward the house. "Mr. Furry said it could be a while before he could get away."

I followed Malone inside.

Blaze and Trixie were asleep in a spot of sunlight that slanted through the chintz drapes at the front window.

The room looked the same. Solid, sensible, no-nonsense furniture. The Greyhound pictures on the walls. The photos of Blanche with stars and celebrities.

And yet, the house felt so different without the energetic Blanche. When I'd been there to talk to her after the Greyhound event, she'd been so nervous and on edge. I'd attributed it to the disastrous fund-raiser, but there may have been much more going on.

"I talked to Blanche the day before yesterday, and yesterday morning, she was supposed to meet me for coffee, but she never showed up." I stroked both dogs lightly, waking them. They lifted narrow elegant heads and looked at me. Their soft short fur was warm from the sun.

"Why were you meeting?" Malone stood arms crossed and watched as I gathered a few of Blaze and Trixie's things and looked for a bag to put them in.

I filled him in on the call I'd made to Blanche, her initial denial that she knew the dead guy, and then her admission otherwise. Or at least that's how I'd interpreted Blanche's slip in calling him by his real name.

"She didn't say how she knew him?"

"No, I thought maybe she'd say when we met, but . . . ." I couldn't finish. "How did she die?" I still couldn't wrap my brain around the idea that Blanche had killed herself.

"A combination of alcohol and drugs."

"Really?" No way was Blanche a drinker.

"It looks like not only was she a drinker but also had a bit of a problem with drugs. How long it'd been going on, we don't know. There will be an autopsy."

"Blanche was a Type A on-the-move person. I've never noticed anything that would lead me to believe she had a problem with drugs or alcohol." I shook my head.

"She left a handwritten note that said, 'It's my fault.'" Malone wasn't judging. This was his "just stating the facts" tone.

"Is this case still the FBI's, even if she's the one that killed Victor?"

His laser-like gaze focused on my eyes. "Why do you think she killed him?"

"I don't. But it seems really pretty coincidental that Blanche knew him, and he was killed, and now she's dead."

"Funny you would say that. Dirk Pennick, our guy who was stabbed at the Greyhound event, was a private detective." Malone hesitated as if he wasn't sure how much he wanted to share. "Based on the note, it looks like maybe Blanche LeRue had something to hide."

"I'm sorry. I still can't believe Blanche had a problem with alcohol or drugs." I fidgeted as I packed up a few toys, some dog treats, and the blanket the dogs had been asleep on.

I was sure I wouldn't have missed signs of drug or alcohol abuse.

"Caro, I've seen several suicides in my career, and, with almost every one of them, the friends and relatives say the same thing." Malone rubbed his forehead. "Maybe part of what pushes someone over the edge is hiding their problems from everyone they know."

"Detective, I'm a psychologist." I snapped the leashes I'd found hanging by the door to each of the dog's collars in turn. "I'm trained to notice warning signs. I'm telling you, they weren't there. Even the last time I talked to Blanche, she was upset, but she agreed to meet me."

"If we find any link to the other case, or anything to indicate it wasn't suicide, I promise you we'll follow the trail." Malone took the bag from me and opened the front door.

"Blaze, Trixie, let's go." The two gentle canines tipped their heads and looked at me, dark eyes questioning, and long elegant bodies still. And then finally, apparently deciding it was okay, moved toward me.

I stepped past Malone and outside. Walking the dogs to my car, I was glad I'd left the top up today. Sighthounds and convertibles might be an iffy combination.

Once I had them situated in the back and their bag stowed in the passenger seat, I turned back to Malone. "These two dogs were family to Blanche. She would not have abandoned them."

"Caro, there was a note. A handwritten note."

"I understand."

I understood, but that didn't mean I agreed with his assessment.

The dogs and I drove toward the ARL. Don Furry would take good care of them. I knew Don, and I knew he would.

But it wouldn't be the same.

Blanche, what were you thinking? I wish you could tell me.

ONCE I'D LEFT Blaze and Trixie with Don, I felt better. He'd already made arrangements with a foster family so the dogs would have some human comfort tonight. Also, he had been given access to some of the files at Greys Matter by Diana Knight and was working with the volunteers there to find a permanent adoptive home for the two.

I only had one more quick appointment—a follow-up—and then I wanted to check in with Diana.

I made my stop to check in with a newer client with a young bluetick Beagle whom I'd seen a couple of weeks ago. Gustav was high energy and needed more exercise than he'd been getting, a common problem in the pampered world of Doggie and Me yoga, puppy strollers, and dog "pawlish." It seemed I constantly found myself preaching "a healthy dog is an exercised dog."

I was mostly following up to make sure Gustav's owner had kept up the exercise routine. I've found, just like with us humans and our exercise intentions, it's good to give some goals. It's easy to start out strong and then to lose momentum.

Gustav's family had done pretty well. I encouraged them to keep going and scheduled another follow-up visit.

Next up, I took PCH to Ruby Point and checked in with Tucker at the guard shack.

I drove to Diana's, still thinking about what Malone had told me. Her house was a castle that somehow managed to look like a cottage. Flowerbeds lush with colorful blooms lined the drive.

I rang the doorbell, and her housekeeper answered.

"Hello, Bella, how is she?" I asked.

"She is doing well, considering." The dark-haired Bella automatically put one leg out to stop the little Puggle, Mr. Wiggles, and

Barbary, Diana's one-eyed Basset Hound, from heading out the door on a grand adventure.

"Is she up to company?"

"Oh, yes." Bella's soft and musical Spanish lilt echoed the warmth of her smile. "Your company especially." She winked, her dark eyes dancing.

"I guess I'd better come in then, before we have any more attempted escapees." I laughed as a Maine Coon cat slipped around Bella's extended leg and eyed the open door.

"Yes, go on through." Bella reached down and nabbed Miss Kitty. "She's in the kitchen."

Diana's kitchen was a big country kitchen with cheery yellow walls and all kinds of room. She had a nice formal dining room, but more often than not, she ate at the large oval oak table or out on her patio. Diana lived alone, having outlived several husbands. And though she cared for Dino and he was clearly crazy about her, I think she liked living by herself. It was hardly like she was really alone with the menagerie that shared her space.

"Hello," I called out as I entered the kitchen.

As usual, Diana was done up nicely, at least that's how Grandma Tillie would have said it. I don't think I'd ever seen her when she didn't have it together. Even a while back when she'd spent some time in the Laguna Beach jail, she'd looked like a million bucks.

Today, it was white slacks and a black-and-white sweater set. Makeup on and perfect as usual. The only thing that hinted at how hard the news about Blanche had hit her was the slight sag of her shoulders and a bit of a shake in her hand as she handed me a crystal glass filled with sweet tea.

"Diana, hon, you didn't need to make anything for me." I hugged her. "I know my way around your kitchen."

"I thought you'd stop by." She smiled a faint smile. "I hoped you would."

Her first question was, of course, about Blanche's dogs, and I filled her in on taking Blaze and Trixie to Don Furry and what he'd told me about the foster family.

I'd expected Diana to be sad, and she was, but she was also upset with Malone and company. She wasn't buying the suicide pronouncement any more than I was.

"There's more to this story, Caro, I just know there is." Her voice was as determined as the set of her jaw. "I only wish Blanche were here to tell us."

I wished that, too. Like Diana, I was sure there was more to Blanche's story.

I took a seat at the table, and Diana did, too, sliding a plate filled with Bella-made pastries my way. Having tasted Bella's treats before, I knew better than to take one with the thought that one would be enough.

I slid the tempting plate out of my reach.

"Oh, go on." Diana pushed the plate back across the table. "You tall, gorgeous thing. Your figure can stand it."

"You're so good for my ego, sugar." I caved and picked up a powdered sugar-coated cookie.

"Besides, remember we've got another workout coming up at our 'Be Safe' self-defense class." Diana made a few slicing moves with her arms á la Pajama Betty.

"Yes, we do. Sam had no idea what he'd signed us up for."

"I have to say Betty Foxx has made the class more entertaining than it would have been." Diana took a drink of the coffee she'd poured for herself. "Where do you suppose Melinda found her?"

"I can't imagine, but I'll bet Matt has had to rethink his classroom technique." I nibbled at my cookie.

"I'll bet you're right."

"I thought I'd get a chance to question our instructor after the last class," I noted between bites, "but Matt was surrounded by a whole slew of women who must think they're going to need to disarm a gunman."

We sat quietly for a few minutes.

I reached down and lifted Mr. Wiggles to my lap for a cuddle.

"Your Detective Malone is out of his gourd if he really thinks Blanche LeRue killed herself."

I'd known she'd get back to Blanche's death when she was ready to talk about it. "He says there will be an autopsy, and they'll review all the evidence." I ignored the "your detective" comment.

"Right. I say we don't wait on them. Let's put our heads together. Caro, you're good at this." Diana put her cup down on the saucer with a clank. She crossed the room and rifled through a drawer until she came up with a pen and paper. "Where do we start?"

I didn't think Detective Malone would appreciate our assistance, but at this point, we needed to do something. I wasn't going to discourage the armchair "detecting" if it helped Diana cope with the loss of her friend.

"We start with 'why,'" I said. "It always comes down to 'why', so let's look at the people involved."

Diana made notes as we listed the people who we had questions about. People who might have something to hide.

Eugene had to go first on the list, though neither of us believed he was a killer. He hadn't come forward. In fact, he had run from the police. Twice.

Alana Benda had been hiding her relationship with our self-defense instructor, Matt. I remembered Matt's interest in what I knew about the stabbing when we'd met at the dog park.

There was the attorney, George Thomas, who'd argued with Blanche. A question of billable hours, she'd said, but he'd seemed very angry for it to be something so simple. Diana didn't have a great opinion of the man to begin with, and when I shared what I'd observed, we agreed we had questions about him.

Then there was Blanche. Like Detective Malone had noted, it did look like Blanche had something to hide. What I'd known of Blanche would not put her on the list, but if there's one thing I've found, it's that we may work with someone, see someone every day, even care about someone, and then find out we really don't know them.

I looked at the time and realized I needed to get home to my own much smaller menagerie.

Diana and I agreed to think more about the people who might need to go on our suspect list. I helped clear up our dishes and resisted as Diana tried to send treats home with me.

I FED MY CREW and then fed myself. I turned on the news, but there was nothing about Blanche LeRue's death.

As Dogbert and I took our evening walk, the sun was setting. I still felt unsettled about Blanche's death and couldn't help but wonder if there was a link to the man who had been killed at the rescue event.

So Dirk Pennick was a private detective? What was he investigating? Whatever it was had gotten him killed. Someone had something to hide that was worth killing to keep hidden. And it looked like there were a number of names on the growing list of people with something to hide.

I reviewed in my head the list that Diana and I had made.

There were at least a couple of people on the list whom I could easily get to and ask a few pointed questions. Tomorrow, I would continue my visits with Greyhound owners. I'd just moved Dave and Alana Benda to next on my follow-ups.

Chapter Twenty

THE FACT THE man who'd been killed had been a private detective shone a whole new light on everyone who'd been keeping secrets.

I called Alana Benda as soon as I thought she'd be up, and told her I'd be stopping by to check on her dogs. I didn't really give her an option. I didn't actually think Alana and Dave Benda's dogs had problems left over from the Greyhound event. They'd appeared to be fine when I'd seen them briefly at the Koffee Klatch. But the follow-up was the perfect ploy to get a chance to talk to Alana without tipping her off.

And I'd still make my report on the dogs I'd already seen, even though there was no Blanche to receive the report.

Alana answered my knock wearing workout clothes. "Oh hi, Caro." She opened the door to let me in, but left it open when she walked away. I closed it and followed her.

The dogs were perched on a chair that'd been placed by the window. They turned to look at me as I came in the room and then went back to watching whatever it was they'd been watching outside.

"I'm happy to have you check the dogs over." Alana waved a hand holding a crystal tumbler in their direction. Her ever-present diamond tennis bracelet was absent this morning, and if I wasn't mistaken, she'd had a nip of something alcoholic for breakfast. "But I don't have much time."

"I think Louie and Lexie are fine." I leveled a look her way.

"Don't you need to examine them or something?" She looked at the dogs still watching out the window.

"I really came by today because I wanted to talk to you."

"Caro, I'd like to chat with you, but maybe we could do lunch or something another time."

Oh great, she thought this was a social visit. "I wanted to ask you about Matt Bjarni."

She went still, her aqua eyes wide.

I thought that would get her attention. "I didn't know the two of you were close."

"Wha—?" Her sharp intake of breath let me know I'd hit the mark.

"I saw you two at La Mie." I watched her face for reaction. "It appeared you are very good friends."

"Yes, friends. That's all, we are just friends."

"A friend you'd rather your husband didn't know about? I'd just left the office a few minutes before I saw you, and Dave told me you had an appointment at The Spa."

"I did. That's right." She went to take a sip from her glass but realized it was empty. "But the appointment got canceled and I was sitting alone, and Matt was having lunch and we were both alone, and so we were talking about my workout and . . . ."

I let her ramble until she was out of breath.

"Did you know the man who was killed at the Greyhound event was a private detective?"

"Who?"

"The dead man. He was a private detective."

"I can't imagine why a private detective would be stabbed, but they know who did it, don't they? Wasn't it that young waiter? That's who the police have been looking for, right?"

She hadn't really answered me.

"And now Blanche is dead." I waited again for reaction.

"I heard she offed herself."

Well, boy howdy, no grief there.

"Apparently the police think she did, but I sure don't think she seemed suicidal."

"You never know, do you?" Again, no regret in her voice. "I really need to get going. So, if we're done here?"

She was definitely in a hurry to get somewhere.

Alana walked to the door and held it open. I could take a hint. We were apparently done talking.

I stopped in the doorway. "You and Matt—"

"Not your concern." Alana gripped my arm and gave a little push so I found myself on other side of the threshold. "Leave it alone." And the door slammed shut.

The woman was strong. As for motive, I didn't know that I'd found out anything of substance, but at the first opportunity I'd share what I knew with Detective Malone.

I still wasn't sure the supposed suicide wasn't going to end up in the Feds' court, but for now, it was a gray area.

So I'd go with the devil I knew.

Chapter Twenty-One

I LEFT THE BENDA residence with Alana's odd behavior on my mind.

Also, a day later, I was even more firmly convinced Blanche LeRue had not committed suicide. And my view was more than what Malone had flagged as simple denial. I was familiar with the denial friends and family often went through, but in Blanche's case, there were no signs of alcoholism or drug abuse. I'd been in her home. It was a matter of convincing Malone her death warranted further digging.

Ollie Hembry was next on my list for the day, and as I drove to Ruby Point, I went over the last conversation I'd had with Blanche. "It's complicated," she'd said.

It sure as shootin' is, Blanche, honey.

It remained to be seen who'd hired Dirk Pennick. Someone had. Could Dave have hired him to investigate Alana? Could someone have hired him to investigate Blanche? But who? And, if so, what for?

I wondered if the FBI had found anything in the house he'd rented to indicate who he was working for and what he was investigating. It seemed to me the answers to those questions were the key to not only why he'd been killed, but also what had happened to Blanche.

I pulled off of Pacific Coast Highway and into the entrance of Ruby Point.

"Good morning, Tucker." I checked in once again with the guard at the gate and drove directly to Ollie's. His property was not far from Diana's, but had nothing of the storybook look of hers. He had asked me to drop off some of my gluten-free dog snacks for one of his pooches who was on a special diet.

I looked forward to Ollie and his brood. He was a kind-hearted man even though he often hid it behind his wild-rocker throwback attitude.

When I rang the doorbell, "God Save the Queen" rang out, but there was a long pause before Ollie eased open the door.

He peeked out from the doorway. "Oh, it's you, luv." His long black hair was loose, and he was dressed in his usual black shirt, black jeans, dark glasses. Today, he'd added a black satin bathrobe to the ensemble. The look worked for him. "Come in, come in."

He edged the door open a bit more, and I slipped inside.

"Are you okay?" I worried about him.

His agoraphobia, which kept him from leaving his house, had been limited to only a fear of being out in public. He'd always been fine with people who came to his home. However, sometimes anxiety disorders can morph into other issues.

"I'm fine, duck." He pushed his blue-tinted sunglasses up on his nose. "I have someone I'd like you to meet."

With Ollie, that kind of statement probably meant he'd added another animal to his menagerie. He was very close to giving Diana a run for her money on the live-in rescue front. I wondered what kind of canine he'd adopted this time.

"Ta-da!" he announced as we walked into the living room.

I'd looked at floor level, watching for some new fur baby to come racing forward, so it took me a minute to raise my eyes to the person sitting on the couch.

"Eugene." I choked on his name. "What are you doing here?"

It was a dumb question. It was clear what he was doing at Ollie's was hiding. The police would not have thought to look for him at Ollie's, and I hadn't thought to mention to either Malone or Agent Milner that Ollie and he knew each other.

"Ms. Lamont, Ollie here persuaded me to talk to you." Eugene swallowed hard, his young face pale. "I didn't kill Dirk, but I don't trust the police."

"Bloody coppers," Ollie interjected.

Ollie'd had a few run-ins himself with law enforcement back in his wild party days, and there was no love lost there. It made sense Eugene would have picked Ollie as an ally.

"Oh, Eugene, hon. You need to talk to the FBI."

"The FBI?" He sat up straight. "What do the Feds have to do with this?"

"You hadn't heard?" I looked from him to Ollie. "The investigation is no longer a local thing. The FBI has taken over the case."

"Haven't had the telly on." Ollie waved a beringed hand. "All bad news in the world of late. Eugene's been helping me sort out some techie stuff."

"In any case, Eugene, you're not doing yourself any favors by hiding. You need to tell the FBI what you know."

"Bloody coppers." Ollie didn't have much new to add, but at least he was consistent in his view.

By this point, Eugene had gotten up from the couch and begun to pace the room. "They'll arrest me. I can't afford a lawyer. Everyone has already decided I'm guilty."

"Eugene, I believe you, and I'll help you get an attorney if you need one." I really meant what I said. It was clear to me Eugene hadn't killed Dirk. There was more to this than an argument over being recognized at a party.

"I don't know, I don't know, I don't know." He mumbled and paced.

Ollie watched him. He reached down to pat Morkie, the little Lhasa Apso and Poodle mix, who'd sidled up next to him.

"Eugene, two people are dead." I stood and caught his sleeve. "If you're not willing to go to the FBI or the police, at least call them and tell them what you know. You can use my phone."

The younger man turned to Ollie. "What do you think?"

"I think Caro is stand-up. If she says she'll help you, she will."

Eugene suddenly made a decision. "Okay, I'll talk to your FBI guy. But I want to call from your phone. And I don't want to do it from here. I don't want to get Ollie in trouble."

"Ah, no worries, mate." Ollie patted him on the back.

"Okay, let's do this." Eugene headed for the door.

Eugene got in the car with me, and we drove just outside the Ruby Point entrance. I felt safe. Even if I'd misjudged the young man— and I didn't think I had—Tucker, in the guard shack, was just a holler away.

And while I hadn't quite perfected Diana's horror movie scream, I could darned well make some noise if I needed to.

Chapter Twenty-Two

EUGENE LOOKED like he'd head for the hills if he could, and Agent Milner looked like he hadn't slept in days.

We sat in the shade on some ornate benches near the Ruby Point guard shack. Milner was back to his usual gray suit, white shirt, tie, and wingtips. The suits surely didn't come off the rack looking that rumpled, but I'd never seen them otherwise. His silver hair was combed, but just barely, and his eyes had bags the like of which I hadn't seen since I'd last seen Grandpa Montgomery's old coon dog.

He handled Eugene with a calm and, dare I say, a kind demeanor.

Probably an FBI interrogation technique.

I guessed it was the most effective technique for someone like Eugene. Probably for a tough guy, Milner would adopt more of an in-your-face attitude.

Could be the FBI Agent was just a nice guy, but I was betting on technique. But then, like Diana frequently points out, I'm a cynic.

I sat quietly and observed, hoping they'd forget I was there. It seemed they had. Agent Milner was good. He pulled information from Eugene little by little, like he had all the time in the world.

He also baited Eugene with bits of info. I'd learned a lot so far about what was actually going on and why the FBI was involved in what had initially been a local murder case.

As they talked, the crumbs Agent Milner threw out gave me a clearer picture. The FBI had never seen Eugene as a suspect. They'd always been after bigger fish.

Eugene had no idea what Dirk had been working on or who he was working for. When he'd seen him at the Greyhound fund-raiser, he immediately thought the man was involved in some big con. And maybe he had been.

"We searched the house Dirk Pennick had been renting at Mission Point, but nothing there indicated who he was working for. No notes, no files."

"I'm not surprised." Eugene bounced his jean-covered leg as he talked. "He was a smart guy, always kept a lot of information in his head."

"Still, houses in that neighborhood aren't cheap, and I don't think Dirk was independently wealthy. So there was either a client, or a scam." Milner was still on a fishing expedition.

"When we argued that night at the dog deal, he claimed he'd gone legit." Eugene's voice trembled. "But I figured he was saying that so I wouldn't out him."

"Do you know of anyone else Dirk Pennick hung out with or anyone he may have simply mentioned?"

"No, I don't." His pale face was flushed. "Wait." His leg stopped bouncing.

Agent Milner waited patiently.

"There was this guy, Joe, we both knew. He was in the work release program at the same time we were both there. Right before I was out of probation. But I don't know where he is or what he's doing now."

"Listen, Eugene, we know the trouble you got into was probably just a youthful prank." Agent Milner paused. "And we're prepared to clear your record in exchange for your help with this. We've hit nothing but dead ends."

"What would I have to do?" Eugene's expression was wary. He was a cynic, too. Too young to be cynical, but life would do that to you.

"Can you talk to any of the guys that were there with you and Dirk? Some of them may have been in contact with him."

Eugene hesitated. His trust in Agent Milner had grown. "That's what I've been trying to tell everybody. I don't hang with any of the guys who got me into that crap."

"I'm not asking you to hang out with them again." Again, Milner's voice was kind and soothing. "But they are not going to talk to someone who looks like me. And"—he paused and glanced my way—"I don't think I can sufficiently disguise myself so they wouldn't know I was law enforcement."

I mouthed, "Not funny."

He calmly went back to Eugene. "You, however, can call, claim the police are looking at you for his murder, and see what they know."

Eugene hesitated and then said, "I can do that."

"All right, young man." Milner tone was soft but stern. "I'm not going to arrest you, but you must not leave the area. Do you understand?"

Eugene nodded.

"By the way, where have you been the past few days?" Milner asked. Again that offhand non-threatening approach.

"With friends."

"Which friends?"

Eugene shook his head. Apparently, he was not going to give up Ollie to "the bloody coppers." I thought probably Ollie could handle it if he did, but Agent Milner didn't press.

They both stood.

"All right, here's my number." Milner handed a business card to Eugene. "You call me with whatever you learn. No matter how trivial it seems."

"Okay." Eugene shoved the card into his jeans pocket.

The FBI agent held out his hand, and he and Eugene shook on it.

"Now, can I give you a ride someplace?" He patted the younger man on the back.

I cleared my throat. "I'm going back to my office, and your sister will be there. You're welcome to come along, if you like," I offered.

"That would be great." Eugene sounded relieved. He was going to cooperate, but he didn't look like he really wanted to spend any more time chatting with Milner.

I unlocked the doors on the convertible so Eugene could get in, but paused before I joined him. "Agent Milner?"

He'd already started toward his vehicle. A very large, very boring sedan. He turned. "Yes?"

"Any progress made in locating my property?" I had to press.

"By that you mean this family brooch?"

"Yes. Have you located it?"

"It was logged into federal evidence, so it's probably at the regional facility." He sighed. "I have someone looking into it. We'll find it."

"I hope so, Agent Milner." I didn't mean to bust his chops, but seriously, how secure was their evidence system if it was that hard to find? More likely, my brooch simply didn't rank high on anyone's to-do list.

As he walked away, he muttered, "I hope so, too."

"Thank you, sugar." I called after him.

THE DRIVE TO downtown Laguna was quiet, although I'd glanced at my passenger a couple of times. I parked the Mercedes in the office lot, but before we got out, I turned to Eugene. "I know you're probably second-guessing yourself at this point. But you did the right thing." I could see the doubt in Eugene's eyes.

"Guess we'll find out." He opened the car door and unfolded his lanky form.

We entered the office, and I knew the exact moment Verdi spotted her brother even before I could see her. The offices a block away probably heard her squeal of delight.

"Eugene!" She flew out from behind the desk and grabbed him in a tight hug. "Are you okay?"

"Sis, yes, I'm fine." He laughed.

"What's going on?" Verdi spotted me behind him. "Are the police coming?"

"No," He peeled his sister's arms from his waist. "I made a deal with the FBI. I'm helping them."

"Really?" Verdi finally let go and stepped back to look him up and down.

"Yes, really." Eugene quickly filled her in on where he'd been and his conversation with Agent Milner.

"Caro suggested maybe I could stay next door in the house where you're taking care of the Bengal cats."

"You can stay with me." Verdi looked like she was going to hug him again.

"Your apartment's really small, and you have lousy Internet service. I need to be able to get online and try to track down some of the guys I was in jail with."

"I don't know." Verdi bit her lip. It was clear she didn't want to let her brother out of her sight for long.

"Sis, I'm not going anywhere." He gave Verdi's shoulders a quick squeeze. "I won't disappear again."

"If Caro thinks it would be okay with April Mae, the lady who owns the house . . . ." She trailed off.

I didn't point out they hadn't checked with me when Eugene had been hiding at April Mae's before. "I'm sure it will be fine."

In fact, April Mae Wooben would be thrilled if she knew she'd provided help to someone who needed it.

"Then let's get your stuff. I moved it back to my apartment when you disappeared." Verdi had the grace to look sheepish like she suddenly realized the position she'd put me in before.

"Go on." I shooed them out the door. "There's nothing going on here anyway."

There was no one else in the office except for Dave Benda.

I wondered how much he'd heard and if the noise had bothered him, but when I glanced in his office, he had his head down, working on his computer.

Crunching numbers.

Dave was always crunching numbers.

Chapter Twenty-Three

THE FBI DIDN'T include me in their briefings, so I had to use other means to get updates on the case.

Eugene had met with the FBI again once he'd made contact with Joe, the guy he'd mentioned from the work release program. He'd filled in the progress for Verdi who stopped by to let me know the latest.

It had been a great move on Agent Milner's part to use Eugene. He was able to collect quite a bit of intel about Dirk Pennick.

It turned out what Pennick had been investigating had nothing to do with any of the wealthy people who were at the Greyhound fund-raiser. The FBI had been barking up the wrong tree. He'd been investigating the Greyhound rescue itself.

Verdi sprawled on my couch and munched on the Portabella mushroom "burger" I'd grilled for dinner. She'd shown up unannounced, but I always made too much. It's the bane of those of us who live alone. I always make too much food.

She spoke between bites. "Eugene says the FBI guy was really happy with what he'd been able to find out."

"Did he say who they were focusing on?"

"They think Blanche LeRue was involved." Verdi finished and got up to take her plate to the kitchen. "Something to do with the finances, that's why the Feds are involved."

"But Blanche told me she paid little attention to the money the rescue collected." I still wasn't convinced about Blanche's role. "She was all about the dogs."

"I guess they don't think she 'acted alone.'" Verdi made little quotation marks in the air. "Someone at the rescue must have been in on it with her."

"That leaves very few suspects." I followed her to the kitchen. "Blanche was the executive director, Dave Benda is their accountant, George Thomas is their attorney." I wished I had a clearer picture of what it was the FBI thought Blanche had done. "The rest are volunteers, and then, of course, there's the board."

"Eugene said the FBI is looking into everyone's background who has anything to do with the rescue." She rinsed her dish and stacked it with mine in the sink, right at home.

"I'd think background checks wouldn't be too difficult for such a small group." I poured us each a glass of iced tea. I'd brewed a new pomegranate raspberry green tea from the Koffee Klatch that Verdi had suggested I try.

She took a sip. "This is good."

We carried our drinks back to the living room. There'd been such a change in Verdi since her brother had come forward. She was more like her old self, and it was nice to have her back.

"I don't know Dave or the attorney that well, but the other board members are all people who don't need to skim money from a rescue group." I set my glass down on the end table. "Diana and Sam are on the board. Also, Alice Tiburon's the chair. All people we could safely say are 'comfortably well-off,'"

"I guess." Verdi emptied her glass and stood. "I'm going to run next door and check on the cats. And talk to my brother one more time. I'll let you know if I find out anything else."

"Okay, hon." I took the empty glass from her. "You do that."

I transferred the dishes in the sink to the dishwasher and added Verdi's glass. I'd grown fond of Verdi. She was a good kid. So was Eugene. I hoped his cooperation with the FBI worked out and he was able to get his record cleared.

Kitchen cleaned, I poured another glass of iced tea, picked up the book I'd started over a week ago, and settled into my favorite chair. It was a thriller by Sandra Brannan, one of my favorite authors, but I'd had a little trouble concentrating on fiction lately. Real-life murder and mayhem will do that to you.

I'd no sooner opened the book and located where I'd left off than the doorbell chimed. Maybe Verdi was back with some new information on the case.

I set my book aside and went to the door. Agent Milner, Detective Malone, and another man stood on my step.

Milner was attired in his usual FBI uniform, a business suit. Malone, his standard, dark jeans, dark T-shirt, leather jacket. The third man was more casually dressed but still had a law enforcement air about him.

Bloody coppers. I heard Ollie's voice in my head, and it made me smile.

No matter. I sincerely hoped one of them had Grandma Tillie's brooch.

"Wow. Please come in." I opened the door wider. "To what do I owe this honor?"

"Ms. Lamont." Agent Milner stepped through first.

"Caro." Detective Malone was next. It had taken a while to get him to call me by my first name, but I was glad to see we'd definitely made the transition.

"I'm Nick." The next guy held out his hand. He was clearly law enforcement but a young pup.

Had I become a part of some training exercise? The "how to return property to an irate citizen" module?

"Hello, Nick." I shook his hand. "Come on in."

The other two were already in and had seated themselves in my living room. Apparently, this wasn't going to be a quick visit.

"Can I get you all something to drink? I have coke, iced tea, wine." I looked from one to another.

"No. No, thanks," they each answered.

"Well then, could one of you tell me what you're doing here?"

Agent Milner kicked it off. "Eugene has had some luck in getting in touch with people he was formerly incarcerated with. We've done some follow-up already and need your help to go further in the investigation."

"What kind of help?" I barely got the words out before the doorbell rang again. "Excuse me while I answer that."

I opened the door this time to Sam who carried a stack of paperwork.

"Hello, Caro." He kissed me on the cheek and followed me to the living room. He didn't seem shocked to see the others.

"You all know each other?" I asked, before returning to my chair. My sarcasm was not at all subtle. Nor did I mean for it to be.

Everyone nodded manly nods. I truly didn't believe my living room had ever contained so much testosterone at one time.

Sam perched on the arm of my chair. "Here's what I found in going through the board reports."

They all leaned forward. It was like they were continuing a conversation they'd started earlier. And I guessed they probably were.

"I don't have access to the accounts themselves," Sam continued.

"Only Blanche LeRue, George Thomas, and Dave Benda have access to those. But my grandmother kept hard copies of the quarterly financial reports provided to the board."

I looked around the room. I was the only one who was lost.

Sam handed out some papers. "If you take a look at the last two years, everything seems to be in order." He flipped a legal-sized page over and pointed. "However, if you go back three years, there's clearly a difference."

"Missing money?" Milner asked.

"It's hard to say without all the details."

"Not enough," Milner said.

"Can someone fill me in?" If they were going to meet in my living room, I was darned well going to be in on this discussion.

Malone spoke up. "Eugene was able to find out that Dirk Pennick, aka Victor Lustig, was investigating Greys Matter. He had stumbled onto something big, and that something got him killed."

Milner picked up the story; a corner of his mouth lifted in a half-smile. "He'd told a friend that he'd been hired to look into things and that he'd discovered a scam of some sort. Nothing like a con man to uncover a scam."

"Our minds aren't as devious. We don't think twisted enough," Malone observed.

"What I've found in the old reports would support that idea." Sam folded the paper he held in half.

"Here's the rub." Agent Milner looked at me. "We're pretty sure, but not absolutely certain, that it wasn't just Blanche LeRue."

"But—" I started to protest.

"I know you don't think Blanche's death was a suicide. Detective Malone has apprised us of your opinion." He looked over at Malone.

I met Malone's stare. I had not changed my mind.

"Here are the facts." He ticked them off on his fingers. "Blanche is dead, she can't tell us the whole story, and the only one who can is the other person who was involved."

"And who is that?"

"That's the problem, as Mr. Gallanos noted, there's a limited lineup of people who have account access. We don't know which one was the accomplice."

"So why not just bring them all in? For Pete's sake, two people are dead." It seemed pretty straightforward to me.

"That would be one approach." Agent Milner held my gaze, but I could sense all eyes on me. "The problem is, as soon as we make a move in cases like this, the suspects disappear. These are people with resources."

I turned to look at the men seated around my living room. There was a reason they were all here.

"If we can act quickly enough and bring them in for questioning, we can prevent the flight, but they immediately lawyer up." He shifted toward me. "And, here's the deal, we're not just interested in this little issue." He tapped the papers Sam had given him. "We believe this may be part of a larger operation we've been tracking. If so, this is only one of many set ups by this group. We want Big Al, the guy who is replicating this all over the country. He's a regular franchise. We want to take him down."

"Big Al?" I couldn't wrap my brain around the idea of some guy named "Big Al" pulling the strings at the pet rescue. Could it be these men had watched too many gangster movies?

"We could access the rescue computer and try to sort it out, but anything could tip them off." Milner looked at me.

"I've had brief discussions with Dave Benda and George Thomas under the pretense of following up on Blanche LeRue's suicide." Malone spoke from where he sat, foot on knee, beside the young man, who'd so far had nothing of substance to add.

I thought about how nervous Dave had been when I'd told him about Blanche not showing up for our meeting. But then I also remembered how livid George Thomas had been when he slammed out of the Greys Matter office the day I'd stopped in there.

"We think Dave Benda is our guy." Milner rubbed his chin with his thumb.

"Dave is Big Al?" I couldn't see it. Dave Benda was a numbers guy, not a mastermind. The only thing he cared about was making enough money to keep his trophy wife in diamonds.

"No, but we believe Dave was Blanche's accomplice and he knows who Big Al is," Milner answered. "We need someone who can get close to Dave without spooking him and offer him a deal. If he will act as an informer, and give us the details, we'll make him an offer that will protect him in exchange for the information he has."

"That's where I come in?" I knew they'd eventually get to why the evening's Bloody Coppers Anonymous meeting was at my house.

Sam spoke up from beside me. "You and Diana."

Young Nick spoke for the first time. "We would send you both in completely wired. It's good to have two people in case of technical problems."

"We also believe having a board member there will add some pressure, because he would question your involvement alone," Milner explained. "He knows you both, so asking him to meet you at the rescue's offices won't raise an alarm for him."

"I could tell him I need some files from Blanche's office." I saw where they were going. "Diana would make perfect sense because of her concern for the rescue."

"If we can get some listening devices into the building beforehand we will, but we'll need to move quickly," Nick said to the group.

"Are you sure Dave's not dangerous?" I wasn't concerned so much for myself, but for Diana who I knew wouldn't ask the question.

"There's nothing to make us think he is. He seems to be the numbers guy." Milner sat back in his chair. "If we thought so, we wouldn't do this. We do think he has information, though, that can help us."

"Okey dokey, I'm in." I looked around the room again. "You knew I would be, didn't you?"

Every head nodded.

"You've already talked to Diana, haven't you?" I wasn't sure why I suddenly thought so, but Agent Milner's glance at the floor told me I'd hit the nail on the head.

"Yes, we have." He looked up. "Though we didn't have Mr. Gallanos's board reports until now to confirm our suspicions. We will finalize plans and meet with the two of you first thing in the morning." He stood. "We'd like to do this tomorrow night if we can, before he gets word through Dirk's friends."

The rest stood and filed out in the order they'd come.

Milner first, with a promise to call first thing tomorrow with details. I reminded him that he also had another promise outstanding. Involving my grandmother's brooch.

Malone stopped for a moment before exiting. "Are you sure you're okay with this?" His blue eyes searched my face for hesitation. "You know, you don't have to do this. It's not your fight."

"I know." I patted his sleeve. "I'm sure."

Nick was next. "Nice to meet you, Ms. Lamont." He held his hand out to shake mine. "I've heard a lot about you."

Yeah, I bet.

"Nice to meet you, too, Nick."

"I'm the technical end of this operation, and you have my word, we'll make sure you and your friend are safe."

"Thanks, hon."

I closed the door and turned to the final visitor, who'd hung back when the rest had exited. "Sam, what, in heaven's name, have I gotten myself into this time?"

"Caro, you don't have to do this." He put his arm around my shoulders. "This is not your battle, love. Not yours, not Diana's."

His words echoed Malone's earlier comment.

"Oh, no." I leaned back into Sam's warmth and solidness. "I'm in. Let's take this sucker down."

Chapter Twenty-Four

DIANA WAS AS excited about the sting operation as if she were actually in the movie, *The Sting*.

She was a big fan of Newman and Redford, and I believe had starred in movies with one or both actors. I wouldn't be surprised if she showed up in suspenders and a fedora.

Agent Milner had prepped us for our parts. I was to call Dave and ask him to meet us at Greys Matter. Young Nick would see that we were wired. Milner and several other agents would be close by and would be able to hear everything. We were to lure Dave into talking about the finances, and then bait him by acting like we knew he was involved. Then, if he bit, we were to say the authorities were willing to make a deal with him in exchange for information which could lead them to the big fish. Big Al.

If he didn't take the bait, we were to walk away.

Nick and Agent Milner met us at my house. No suspenders or fedora were in sight. Diana had gone for basic black, as had I. Her outfit was a nice Missoni knit, and mine an Escada. We'd both considered outfits that would easily hide the listening devices.

As soon as we were wired up, Milner gave us final instructions, and we headed to my car and drove straight to the rescue office.

Dave arrived shortly after we got there.

"Don't you two look nice." He opened the office door with a number code and ushered us in. He hadn't actually looked at either of us. "Out for a night on the town?"

I could see Diana's jaw tighten. Compliments are nice, but insincere compliments are worthless, and patronizing compliments are insulting. Why is it some men don't understand that women can hear the difference?

Whoa, Diana sugar, don't let him distract you.

"We may do dinner and a little champagne after this?" I winked at her.

I could see her relax. Dave was oblivious to our byplay. He'd headed down to his office expecting us to follow.

A sense of sadness hit me as I walked down the hallway. I glanced at the Greyhound pictures on the walls. No matter how any of this turned out, Greys Matter had done a lot of good for the dogs. Just a few short days ago, I'd been here talking to Blanche about the Greyhound owners and their dogs. Who could have predicted all that had gone on since that day?

Dave pulled out a chair for Diana and one for me.

He addressed Diana. "You had some questions for me?"

I understood better why Agent Milner and Detective Malone had thought Diana was key. Dave nearly knocked himself over kowtowing to her. And we hadn't even gotten started yet. Some of it was her position in the community, and the other part of it was he was fighting for his job. With Blanche gone, there were bound to be changes at the rescue.

"We do have some questions." I leaned forward, partly to get his attention but mostly because I wanted to be sure the microphone I wore would pick up every word he said.

"About the rescue finances," Diana added.

"What about them?" Dave sat back, his light blue eyes narrowed.

"We believe there are some irregularities." I pulled out one of the papers Sam had provided.

"Where did you get that?" His tone turned hard.

I wished I could see his hands. I knew the FBI agents were close, but if he had a gun in his desk drawer, they'd only be close enough to call an ambulance.

"This is the report you provided to board members quarterly, isn't it?"

"You're not a board member."

"But I am, Mr. Benda." Diana drew herself up in her chair. "And we know you're involved in taking money from this organization."

Dave didn't speak. Belligerence had morphed into shock.

"You'd better come clean." Diana pointed one perfect pink-tipped finger toward him.

I wondered what role she was channeling now. I was awed by her ability to take on a tough persona on cue. This was going down faster than I'd thought it would.

"There's plenty of evidence the FBI has recently uncovered which will implicate you," I said with some fervor. I hoped I played my role as well as Diana. She was an actress; I was a pet therapist. I did my best.

"What evidence?"

"It doesn't matter." I brushed his question aside. "What matters is that you're going to prison for a very long time."

"You took advantage of people who were doing good things. Helping innocent animals." Diana gestured toward the Greyhound pictures on the walls. "These dogs deserve a chance, and you've taken that away."

Dave swallowed hard, but didn't speak.

I felt bad doing it, but desperate times called for desperate measures. Dave's face reflected no regret over the damage he'd done to innocent people or to the Greyhound rescue effort.

No remorse. But I knew his weakness. His fear.

"You're going to prison for a very long time," I repeated, "and I don't think your beautiful wife will spend years alone waiting for you. Everything will be gone, Dave."

He licked his lips, and his eyes turned watery.

Oh, hell's bells, the man is going to cry.

Maybe I'd overplayed my hand.

I looked over at Diana. We both knew the script.

"But here's the thing you need to think about, Dave." I paused. "The FBI is willing to work with you."

"That's right," Diana chimed in. "If you're willing to help them, they'll go easier on you."

"What do they want?" He'd gone white.

I hoped he didn't pass out. "Names."

"What names?" He gulped air.

"Big Al." I watched Dave closely for any sign he was about to either reach for a weapon or bolt. We had a signal we were supposed to use if he tried to run. "They want to know who else was involved in the operation."

Boom! Dave's head went down on his desk.

For a few seconds I thought maybe the man had been shot. That wasn't the case. The man had slammed his head down on his desk and was sobbing uncontrollably.

Holy Freak Out, Batman.

"No one. No one," he cried. "Blanche and me. That's all. No one else."

"Are you sure?" Diana got up from her chair. "No Big Al?"

"I would never work with some Big Al. I don't know anything about that." Dave raised a tear-streaked face and then—*boom!*

Slammed his head back down.

"It was just Blanche and me. I don't have anything to tell them." He mumbled against the desktop and then suddenly raised his head again. "I didn't kill that man. That wasn't me. Blanche did it." He wiped his eyes against his jacket sleeve and then down his head went again.

My eyes teared up. I felt a little sorry for the idiot, but only a little. Blanche? A killer? What an awful mess. When I thought of all the people who'd been taken advantage of and all the animals who'd gone without help because of Dave's greed and Blanche's apparent addictions, I was short on compassion. I felt sad for them, but mostly sad for the people they'd used.

I looked over at Diana and could see the same emotions reflected on her face.

When I looked up, Agent Milner stood in the office doorway, a couple of other agents behind him.

"You two all right?"

We each nodded.

"Cuff him and put him in the car," he told the others. "Then send the team in here to pack up this office."

They led Dave out.

"Well, there you have it." I looked around. "Not exactly what you wanted, but at least we have answers about why Dirk was investigating and why he was killed."

"That's right." Agent Milner's tone was neutral, which I now knew was pretty much default mode for him. He couldn't be happy. The sting had turned out to be a dead end on his big case, but I imagined dealing with dead ends was part of the job. "Let's get you two ladies outside and let Nick unwire you." He held the door for open.

Diana and I stepped outside where the block had collected a line-up of police cars and other official vehicles. Nick waited by a van. I'd be glad to get the listening devices removed. They were light and not difficult to have on, but it was a little creepy knowing everything you said was being recorded.

Nick had us free of wires in a short time. The Laguna Beach police department had cordoned off the area, but Dino was allowed through to speak to Diana. I spotted Sam near one of the FBI sedans talking with one of the agents and headed in his direction.

When he saw me, he left the man standing there and ran to me.

He grabbed me in a hug and lifted me off my feet. Once he put me down, he cupped my face and searched my eyes. "Are you okay?"

Milner's question from earlier, but with much more intensity.

"Yes." I smiled at him. "I was never really in harm's way, sugar."

"Not physically perhaps, Caro, *agapi mou*. But this was an ugly business." The man had a way of zeroing in on the heart of things.

"Seriously, Sam." I hugged him hard. "I am okay. Go finish what you were in the middle of."

It seemed like forever, but was probably no more than thirty minutes and the FBI's work was done. Dave's office was packed up and the boxes loaded into a van to be taken for the financial forensics team to review. Dave was off to Orange County to be booked. Malone had drawn the short straw and was on his way to notify Alana that Dave wouldn't be home for dinner.

As for the rest of us, we were free to leave. Dino offered to take Diana home and she accepted. I was kind of glad. We could rehash the evening later. I was more than ready for my sweats, a bowl of popcorn, a good light-hearted movie, and a snuggle with my furry roommates.

I'd bragged about enjoying a glass of celebratory champagne earlier, and Sam had offered, but I truly was plain old exhausted.

Chapter Twenty-Five

IF YOUR CURIOSITY says one thing and your common sense says something else, you should always listen to your common sense.

The street was deserted when I slipped back into the Greys Matter offices using the code I'd watched Dave use earlier. Everyone was gone; Dave Benda had confessed. But something wasn't right.

There were a dozen reasons to think the FBI had the right guy. Dave Benda had access to the rescue's books of account. There was no reason to doubt his claim that Blanche had given him a portion of the money he'd helped her embezzle from the Greyhound rescue. A look into his finances and the rescue's books would confirm it.

He would be prosecuted for being a party to the mishandling of the rescue's funds. Blanche would be on record as the one who'd killed Dirk Pennick and then herself. Case closed.

But I was still worried we'd missed something important. Mainly, I was still bothered by Blanche's suicide. So much didn't jive. The carefully written suicide note when she'd told me she always used her tablet computer because her handwriting was awful. Leaving Blaze and Trixie.

Was it possible Dave was the killer and not Blanche? We knew he was a liar. Why couldn't he have lied about that? It wasn't as if Blanche were here to contradict him.

Was it possible Alana was the killer and Dave confessed to protect her? Especially if the detective had uncovered the funny business between her and Matt Bjarni. Matt had even said a woman could have done the deed. Come to think about it, he'd had a lot of questions that day at the dog park.

I tried to picture Alana stabbing Victor. The con man had not been a big man. I knew because I'd been up close with him. A strong woman could have done it. The FBI believed that a woman had and that woman was Blanche.

I sat down at Blanche's desk and thought.

Who else could have had a reason to kill Victor, aka Dirk?

I pictured all the people at the event and tried to recall what they'd said about their interactions with Dirk that night. Many of them had told lies or, at the very least, only partial truths.

Eugene had words with Dirk about being there. Verdi's brother had failed to mention his record, but I better understood why now. The one good thing to come out of this was Eugene getting a fresh start.

Blanche had said she didn't know Dirk, but she had in fact talked to him earlier in the week.

Dave had also claimed to not know him, but of course he would lie if the private detective's investigation had led him to Dave's unscrupulous accounting.

Who else had mentioned seeing him at the event? Diana had heard of him but hadn't met him until that night. Alice Tiburon mentioned seeing him and Eugene come in from outside. Which was a big part of why the police immediately focused on Eugene.

Wait a minute. If Victor had been outside, his clothes would have been wet. I remembered noticing the raindrops on Tova Randall's already dewy skin. But when I had grabbed his arm and he had fallen against me, his suit wasn't damp at all.

Why would Alice lie about seeing Victor coming in from the outside? A silly thing, really, to lie about.

I sat up quickly, and as I did, I felt something jammed into the cushion of Blanche's chair. It was the small tablet computer she'd always carried. How had they missed it? I'd need to get it to Agent Milner. It might hold some information that would help.

It was probably dead, but I hit the power button anyway. It came on. I looked at the screen and wondered what answers it might hold. One of the apps was the one Blanche and I had used to update the spreadsheet of Greyhound owner visits. I wondered what other information or documents she might have shared. And with whom.

Dang it. A password was needed.

I tried a couple of guesses and then sat back. Anyone with the love Blanche had for her dogs would use a dog reference. Blaze and Trixie. TrixieBlaze. BlazeTrixie. Blaze&Trixie. It took me only a few tries for the right combination and there it was. I opened the document titled "Pennick Detective Agency" and read through quickly. As I did, all the pieces fell together.

Hold your ponies, people. Blanche hadn't killed the private detective.

She was the one who'd *hired* him. He'd uncovered a money-laundering operation that'd been going on for more than a year.

Blanche had not killed Dirk.

Blanche had not killed herself.

Not only that, Big Al wasn't a man, but a woman.

"Oh, wow." I said to the empty office. I reached for my phone to call Agent Milner.

"So you figured it out?"

I whipped the chair around as Alice Tiburon stepped out of the shadows and into the office.

"It was always you, wasn't it?"

"It was." She wasn't taking any chances with a carving knife tonight; her long, elegant, perfectly-manicured fingers were wrapped around a small handgun.

"You were using the rescue to launder money." It wasn't a question. The document detailing the findings was clear.

"The perfect setup. Dave was hungry for extra cash to keep his fancy trophy wife happy, Blanche was so busy with the rescue she wasn't paying attention to accounting, and all you people crazy about saving the stupid dogs kept the money coming through. Easy to hide and process hundreds of thousands over time."

"Until Blanche got worried and hired a private detective," I pointed out.

"Yes, Blanche and her detective. A man who'd been in prison, no less."

"That's the trouble with ex-cons." I shrugged. "They know where the dirt is, and they aren't afraid to dig."

A movement behind Alice caught my eye.

I could see the hallway and reception area in the mirror, just like Blanche had been able to see the front desk the day I'd come to see her at the office.

And I could see Diana tiptoeing closer and closer.

"So what are we to do now, Alice?" I kept her talking to cover any sound. "Or should I call you 'Big Al?'"

"I'd hoped to take care of things earlier when I found out Dave was meeting you. A nice murder-suicide was the plan. Poor Dave would shoot you and your Hollywood has-been friend, and then, filled with remorse, sadly shoot himself." Her red lips lifted in a sneer.

Hollywood has-been?

I heard Diana's sharp intake of breath at the comment, but thankfully, Alice was too busy waving her gun around and telling me how I was going to die.

"But then something didn't smell right about that setup. So, dimwit Dave was coached on exactly what he was to say if he was caught. I'll have him out in no time." She smirked. "Poor bleeding-heart Blanche will take the fall for everything. After all, she's not here to defend herself."

"The FBI has all of the rescue's books of account. I think their forensic team is pretty smart."

"All they have is the dummy evidence I had Dave create."

Well, don't knock yourself over patting yourself on the back, sugar.

"And what about me?" I asked.

"Don't worry, Pet Shrink, I have something planned for you." She motioned with the gun. "Give me that computer."

I stepped from behind the desk, held it out to her, and took a full step forward.

Right on cue, a shrill scream pierced the air.

You know the one. Ear-splitting horror movie, *I-Married-a-Zombie* scream.

That was my signal. I quickly moved to the side, grabbed the muzzle of the gun, slapped Alice's forearm, and took the weapon. Just like in class.

Matt would have been proud.

Alice was stunned.

Frankly, I was stunned too. Just a little.

"Great job, Caro." Diana stepped where Alice could see her. "Hollywood has-been, huh?"

Diana looked like she'd like to try out a few more of the moves we'd learned in Matt's class. On Alice.

Alice looked like she might make a run for it.

"I wouldn't try it, Alice. The FBI is right outside." Diana lifted her cell phone to her ear. "Did you get all that?"

Suddenly, the office was full of FBI agents.

Agent Milner cuffed a coldly furious Alice and sent her off with one of the other agents.

"Are you okay?" he asked for the second time that night.

My pulse wasn't quite back to normal, and I was a wee bit shaky but yeah, I was okay. "I'm fine."

"What?" He held his hand to his ear. "I can't hear you. I think that scream may have broken my eardrum."

And then Agent Milner actually smiled.

Big Al was in custody. He'd gotten his man, er, woman. All was right with the world.

"It was epic." I grinned.

Chapter Twenty-Six

THIS TIME, THE after party did involve champagne.

Agent Milner and his forensic team had work to do at the rescue office, but there was no need for me to stick around. In fact, Diana and I really needed to get out of the way so they could do their thing.

My house was closest so we decided to meet there to debrief. On the way, I called Sam who joined us. Once home, I called Verdi.

Dino supplied some much-needed food and the champagne. He made himself at home in my kitchen filling plates with fruits, nuts, breads, and cheeses. In the excitement of the evening, we'd all skipped dinner, and so the snacks were welcome.

The doorbell rang. I opened it to Verdi and Eugene who wore big smiles.

"Come in." I hugged her. There were tears in her eyes.

"Caro—I, ah—" Eugene stammered.

I hugged him, too. "Come in," I repeated and pulled them inside.

They joined the group in my living room. Diana had kicked off her shoes and sat on the end of the couch, one leg under her, a pillow at her back.

I settled into my favorite chair, and Dogbert jumped up to sit on my lap. Sam perched on the arm just as he had the previous night, though the mood was much less sober tonight. I looked around the room, my heart full. How lucky was I to be surrounded by such amazing friends?

"So, tell." Verdi dropped into one of the other easy chairs.

I took a deep sigh and rubbed Dogbert's back.

"After Dave was arrested, I was still concerned we'd missed something important and went back to the Greys Matter office," I explained.

"I felt the same worry," Diana added. "I had Dino circle back to the rescue office, and I couldn't believe my eyes when I saw Caro slip inside."

"Oh, wow." Verdi's eyes were wide.

"When I saw Alice Tiburon go in also, I followed her," Diana continued. "And called Agent Milner."

"Thank goodness you did." I leaned back in my chair and snuggled my pooch.

"I didn't really think you were in danger, or I wouldn't have been so calm." Diana laughed.

"I didn't think I was in danger either, or I wouldn't have gone back alone." I shook my head at the risk I'd taken.

"And I didn't think either of you were in danger, or I would not have sat in my car and let you two waltz into the arms of a killer." Dino raised his hands in the air. "It was Alice Tiburon, I thought. I know her. I am sitting in my car, checking email on my phone, thinking you're in there having a nice chat."

"You couldn't have known." Diana smiled at him.

"Then all these police cars come racing up. Oh, *mio Dio!*" Dino clutched his chest. "I almost have a heart attack."

"I was halfway home when you called me and—" Sam stopped and took a deep breath. Then he dropped his hand gently on the back of my neck and leaned forward to kiss the crown of my head.

I smiled up at Sam and reached up to touch his hand. "If it hadn't been for the self-defense course you enrolled us in, we wouldn't have had the moves to take down 'Big Al.'"

"Look out, these are deadly weapons." Diana waved her arms around like Pajama Betty.

I smiled at her. "What a night, huh?"

I still found it difficult to believe all the signs I'd missed, we'd all missed, that should have pointed us to Alice Tiburon.

Dino passed out crystal flutes and filled them with sparkling champagne. I couldn't help but think back to the Fifty Shades of Greyhound event that had started this all. And Victor, or rather Dirk, and his investigation. Hired by Blanche, he must have followed the money which had eventually led him to Dave and to Alice. And had gotten him killed. I had almost become a "Big Al" victim myself. Thankfully, Diana had felt the same uneasiness I had, and had gone back.

I lifted my glass in salute. "here's to friends and rescuers."

We all sipped.

"And"—Sam raised his glass—"here's to the two most courageous women I know."

"Thank you, Sam."

Diana unfolded her legs and stood. "One final toast." She was suddenly serious. "Here's to Blanche and the others like her, who give so much to rescue these wonderful and gentle dogs."

We all raised our glasses in salute.

"Yes," I whispered. "To Blanche and the Greyhounds."

Chapter Twenty-Seven

FBI AGENT JOHN Milner was waiting for me when I got to the office the next morning.

As always, he wore the same slightly disheveled look. A suit and tie that, while good quality, had seen better days. Today, he also wore a very official air.

"Good morning," I greeted him.

He stood as I approached. "Good morning, Ms. Lamont. We really appreciate your assistance and the risks you took to help us with the case." He cleared his throat.

He was a good agent, a smart man, and, I believed, a genuinely nice guy. I felt a little bad about all the grief I'd given him. A little bad.

"I wanted to personally return this." He reached in his suit pocket, pulled out a plastic bag, and handed it to me.

Thank the heavens! Grandma Tillie's brooch.

"Oh my, sugar! Thank you so much." I patted his arm.

I would have hugged him, but I was afraid it would give him a heart attack.

I didn't know what strings he'd had to pull to find it, but the fleeting satisfied smile said he felt like he'd paid his debt.

Opening the bag, I carefully unwrapped the paper swaddling. There'd better not be any damage to the brooch. I lifted the paper away and the pin dropped into my hand. It was a beautifully garish, and expensive piece of jewelry.

What?

"What is this?" I looked up at Milner.

The trinket in my hand was beautifully garish and probably expensive, but it was not Grandma Tillie's brooch.

Shining gold formed delicate pointy ears. A collar of seed pearls wrapped around an elegant neck, brilliant emeralds winked in the eyes, and a ruby button nose sparkled. Sparkling diamond baguettes made up the teeth of the smiling face of a Cheshire cat.

I didn't know how it was possible.

I didn't know how she'd done it.

But one thing I knew for sure was that somewhere my cousin, Mel, was smiling that exact same smile.

The End

Desperate Housedogs

Excerpt

"You'll be howling with laughter!"
—*Kathy Bacus, author of CALAMITY JAYNE*

Desperate Housedogs
Book One, The Pampered Pets Mysteries
By Sparkle Abbey

Crime in Laguna Beach Has Just Gone to the Dogs . . .

When **Caro Lamont**, former psychologist turned pet therapist, makes a house call in posh southern California to help **Kevin Blackstone** with his two misbehaving German Shepherds, she expects frantic dogs, she expects a frantic dog owner, she even expects frantic neighbors. What she doesn't expect is that two hours later the police will find Kevin dead, and that as the last person to see Kevin alive (well, except for the killer), she is suddenly a person of interest, at least according to Homicide Detective **Judd Malone**.

Caro, animal lover and former Texas beauty queen, moved to Laguna Beach for a fresh start after a very nasty and public divorce which ended with the closing of the private counseling practice she and her ex-husband shared. With eleven-thousand dogs—more dogs than kids—Laguna seemed like the perfect spot to open a pet therapy business. And it had been, up until she had to catch a killer by the tail.

Chapter One

I don't normally break into people's homes, but today I was making an exception.

Not wanting to make the burglary too obvious, I'd parked my car down the street and fought through the bougainvillea hedge to the back of the house. In southern California the bougainvillea blooms everywhere, luxurious but tough, like old starlets wearing too much pink lipstick. Determination thumped in my chest, but I was still as nervous as a long-tailed cat in a room full of rockin' chairs. Glancing left and then right to make sure none of the neighbors were around, I flipped up the sand-crusted mat and grabbed the key that lay under it.

My cousin, Melinda, always kept her spare key in the same spot. This particular mat said, "Wipe Your Paws."

Mel's place was nice. Not posh, but very nice even by Laguna Beach standards. Not at all like the open spaces we'd grown up with in Texas but nothing to sneeze at. Palm trees and Jacaranda trees surrounded her patio, and morning was already warming the ocean breeze. I unlocked the door and slipped inside. If I were lucky I'd find my target right away and get out quick. If I were really lucky, it would be a few days before Mel realized the brooch was gone.

I stepped into her sunshine-bright kitchen and noted the stack of dirty dishes. I truly wished the girl wouldn't leave dishes in the sink. Here in the semi-desert you run the risk of bugs. Bugs the size of cocker spaniels.

Eww. I shivered, shaking off the thought like a wet dog shaking off summer rain.

First, I checked the freezer. Not a very original hiding place and not a very effective one either, as I myself had discovered. I'd tried freezer paper and a label that said "Pig Hearts" but Mel had figured it out.

Okay, nothing in there.

Missy, Mel's bulldog, lumbered into the kitchen, her only greeting an eye roll that said, "Oh, it's just you."

I reached down and scratched behind her ears. She leaned into the ear rub. "If only you could talk, sugar. You'd tell me where Mel put it, wouldn't you?"

Missy gave a low, snuffly bark and butted my hand, effectively sliming it. Bulldogs are pretty darn loyal. Could be she wouldn't give up the hiding spot even if she knew. She waddled back to the living room and her spot by the picture window, as if to say, "You're on your own, girl."

"Fine, Missy. You're as stubborn as your mama." I wiped dog drool on my jeans and got back to the task at hand.

Hmmm . . . where would my beautiful (but devious) cousin put the thing? Like a bad Texas summer heat rash, irritation prickled.

Geez Louise, Mel, how long would it have taken to clean up after yourself?

I ran water in the sink and started stacking plates in the dishwasher.

See, that was the problem. Mel's not a bad kid, and only a couple of years younger than me, but she's so dang impulsive it seems I'm always cleaning up her messes. Take Mel's fight with the zoning board over not getting a permit for her new patio or her on-and-off-again relationship with Grey Donovan.

Grey is a prince (in the metaphorical sense) and is caught in the unfortunate position of having befriended two headstrong southern women with a competitive streak. We'd inherited it—the competitive streak, I mean. Our mamas had both been Texas beauty queens, and we'd both lived the pageant life—for a while.

That's to say, until we rebelled. We'd each defied our mothers in our own unique way. Mine a little pushier, but straightforward. Mel's a little wilder and out there. But then that kinda sums up everything y'all need to know about the two of us.

More about that later. Right now I had some searching to do before my cousin came home or her *lovely* neighbors called the cops.

I tried her bedroom, the study (junk room in Mel's case), the bathroom (I was happy to see she was still on her allergy meds), the closet (smaller junk room) and still came up empty-handed. Now, I was back to the kitchen.

Stumped, I stood and looked around, hands on my hips, arms akimbo, mind on hyper drive. It was a funky kitchen but decorated more for fun than utility. Mel's cookie jar was in the shape of a golden retriever. It was just flat adorable, the dog in a playful ready-to-pounce position. I wondered where she'd gotten it. If we were speaking, I'd ask her. But we're not.

I couldn't help it. I shook my finger at the cookie jar. *Melinda Langston, you should not be living on junk food and sweets.*

Her freezer'd been full of microwave dinners and her refrigerator completely devoid of any healthy fruits and vegetables. Probably living on processed food and sugar.

Still, Mel had always been a fabulous cook. She just didn't necessarily follow a recipe. The girl was a bang-up baker though, and cookies were her specialty. My mouth watered. One cookie would never be missed.

Don't mind if I do, cousin. I lifted the dog's butt to help myself and plunged my hand in the cookie jar.

Well, for cryin' in a bucket! Was the dang thing empty?

I couldn't believe I'd made the decision to indulge in empty calories only to be thwarted. I rooted around the inside of the cookie jar, my fingers only touching smooth pottery.

Wait. What was that?

Instead of cookies, my hand connected with metal. Grandma Tillie's brooch. She'd put Grandma Tillie's brooch—*my* brooch—in a cookie jar.

I pulled it out, brushed off the cookie crumbs, and turned it over carefully to check for damage.

Grandma "Tillie" Matilda Montgomery's brooch is the ugliest piece of jewelry you've ever laid eyes on. A twenty-two karat gold basket filled to the brim with fruit made from precious stones. Diamonds, topaz, emeralds, rubies. It is beyond garish.

Garish and gaudy, but significant. In her will, Grandma Tillie had left it to her "favorite granddaughter." I knew she meant to leave it to me. Mel was just as convinced she'd left it to her.

I prodded it with my finger. One of the emeralds might be a teeny bit loose. Promising myself I'd check more thoroughly for damage when I got home, I tucked the brooch in the outside pocket of my handbag and gave it a little pat.

Back with me, where it belonged.

I finished stacking the dishwasher, turned it on, called good-bye to Missy (who ignored me), and let myself out the back. I was just replacing the key when my cell phone rang.

"Hello." I answered in a low tone. No need to alert the neighbors.

I'd made it so far without drawing any attention. Making my way to the front of the house, I walked quickly toward my car.

"Hey, Caro, this is Kevin. Kevin Blackstone." He sounded frantic. But then I'm used to frantic clients. "I need your help."

Oh, I don't think I mentioned it, but I'm Caro Lamont, and when I'm not breaking and entering, I'm the proprietor of Laguna Beach's Professional Animal Wellness Specialist Clinic (the PAWS Clinic for short).

I'm not a dog trainer. Tons of other folks are more qualified in that arena. I basically deal with problem pets, which as a rule involves dealing more with the behavior of the humans than the pet. If I suspect a medical problem I refer pet parents to my veterinarian friend, Dr. Daniel Darling.

I could hear the deep barks of his two German Shepherd dogs in the background. It sounded like Kevin had a problem.

Kevin lived in the exclusive Ruby Point gated community just off of Pacific Coast Highway (fondly referred to as PCH by the locals).

With all the noise, I couldn't hear what it was Kevin needed.

"I'll come by in a few minutes."

I think he said, "okay" but it was difficult to tell over the chaos on his end.

Extremely pleased with myself over the successful retrieval of my inheritance, I climbed in my silver vintage Mercedes convertible. Humming, I thought about the brooch, *my* brooch, safe in my handbag.

It was turning out to be a beautiful day in lovely Laguna Beach.

Life was good.

Chapter Two

The dogs were desperate and so was Kevin.

He was clearly at the end of his rope. Or would that be leash?

Kevin's two German Shepherd dogs circled and barked and circled and barked while the television blasted above the din, and Kevin Blackstone shouted at me.

"They've been at this for two whole days."

That was Kevin.

"Bark. Bark."

"Bark. Bark."

That was the dogs.

"Come in for the spring clearance sale at Orange County European Motors."

The TV announcer.

It had been going on since I'd arrived at Kevin's, and it was enough to make *me* desperate.

"I've tried everything to get them to stop. They continually run to the patio doors, but there's nothing out there." Kevin was a good-sized guy and had a strong grip on their collars, but clearly the dogs were distraught. Kevin looked like he hadn't slept in days.

"Bark. Bark."

"Bark. Bark."

"Breaking news: The body of a man found at Crystal Cove State Park has not yet been identified. Authorities are releasing few details but TV 10 News will talk with hikers who discovered the body."

Kevin continued shouting over the clamor. "I tried letting them outside thinking it was maybe a squirrel or something, but at first they wouldn't go. They just stood in the doorway and growled."

I didn't approach the dogs just yet. "Tell me about what's been going on. Has anything changed in their routine?"

Shepherds aren't a nervous breed. When they bark, they're barking at something.

"No, nothing has changed."

Or at least I think that's what Kevin said.

Between the bark, bark and the "Now we go live to . . . " from the television, I could hardly hear myself think, let alone carry on a conversation.

"Kevin, sugar, would you mind turning the television off?"

"What?"

I pointed toward the super-sized wide-screen TV.

"Oh." He released his hold on the dogs, picked up a manly remote, and clicked the TV off.

I sighed. At least one din-producing item down. The dogs continued to bark, but the noise level was a bit more tolerable.

Okay, where were we?

I'd worked with Kevin's dogs before. About a year ago they'd had a problem with chewing up his new furniture. The doggy therapy seemed to have done the trick. At least the furniture I could see from my vantage point appeared to be intact.

"Tell me again, when did this start?" I asked.

"Two days ago."

"Tell me specifically when you first noticed the dogs' behavior problems."

"Well, I'd been at the gym. I came home, and they came to greet me like they always do. No jumping up."

He saw my raised brow.

"Then they just started going ape-shit. Running to the patio door and then back to me. Patio door—me. Patio door—me." Kevin flung his arms back and forth for emphasis. "I let them outside, and they ran out there. They ran around and barked and then ran back to me. I finally had to bring them inside for fear Mandy next-door would turn me in to the homeowners' association for noise pollution."

Ruby Point was way over the top about their association rules. Apparently Kevin had gotten sideways with Mandy Beenerman, his next door neighbor, a few months ago over a non-conforming mailbox he'd put up. It had been LA Lakers purple and gold, and Mandy, who was a former Celtics cheerleader turned super-snob, had turned him in.

I thought it probably had more to do with spite than good taste. But I could see where Kevin Blackstone might occasionally need a reminder.

To tell you the God's honest truth, I wasn't sure what Kevin Blackstone did for a living, but the same could be said for a lot of my clients. None of my business, you know. All I knew was he lived alone in his huge, multi-level, modern contemporary mansion, and he asked me out at least once a month. I turned him down just as regularly.

While the house was tastefully decorated, I'm certain it had been professionally done with little input from Kevin because he, today as most days, sported really bad plaid shorts paired with a loud orange-colored polo. Who knows, maybe the guy was color-blind.

And me? Who was I to judge? I guess today I sure didn't look like I knew Dior couture from the Dollar Discount store. It would drive my mama insane, but then pretty much everything I did drove her bananas.

Anymore I dressed more for comfort than fashion. Jeans, T-shirt, tennies. My vocation often required rolling around on the ground with puppies or crawling behind ten-thousand-dollar couches to retrieve recalcitrant kitty cats. I loved to get gussied up on occasion, but lately those occasions had been few and far between.

Kevin raked a meaty hand through his reddish hair. "They're always such good dogs. I thought maybe they were just stir-crazy, so I took them for a walk, but drama princess Shar was outside with her dinky dog. She claimed 'her baby' was being traumatized by Zeus and Tommy Boy, and told me if I didn't get my dogs under control, I'd 'be sorry.' Woo, Shar, I'm so scared." Kevin held up his hands and did a fake frightened look.

His neighbor a few mansions down the street, Shar Summers, had a tiny Chinese Crested named Babycakes. For those of you who aren't familiar with the breed, they are delicate, very needy pooches that look more like small alien creatures than dogs. Easily traumatized. A toy poodle would do it, let alone Zeus and Tommy Boy and their bark-fest.

Bottom line, Kevin's housemates were out of control, and if the barking continued there was the distinct possibility someone (probably Mandy) would lodge a neighborhood complaint and Laguna Beach Animal Control could impound the dogs. In lieu of an explanation, we'd start with behavior modification.

"Bring me their treats." I'd been ignoring the dogs. The last thing you want to do when dealing with bad behavior is inadvertently reinforce it. Unfortunately that's exactly what a lot of pet owners do under the mistaken impression they're comforting the animal.

Kevin returned with a box of Bowser Treats from my cousin Mel's shop, the Bow Wow Boutique. Their favorite.

"Okay, here's what we're gonna to do." I picked up one of the treats, closed my hand over it, and turned my back on the dogs.

When they stopped barking, I spun around and gave it to them. It worked only for a moment and then they were back at it.

After a few more tries, I handed the box to Kevin. "You try."

He mimicked my ignore/reward method, and eventually the spans between barking spates increased.

After an hour of working with Zeus and Tommy Boy (and Kevin), I felt like we'd made some progress. I bent and hugged the two dogs, partly to assess their tension and partly because I sincerely liked the guys.

Initially, the times they weren't barking were very few, but eventually there were longer gaps. I tell you, I've worked with a bunch of barkers, and I'd never seen anything quite like it.

"You said you let them out on the patio?"

"I did the first day," Kevin said. "I thought maybe they'd smelled a wild animal or something. But there was nothing. Nothing I could see, anyway."

"Well, let's try it again." Maybe there was a dead bird or squirrel and they'd picked up the scent. Could be it was the nose thing. Their super nose is why German Shepherd dogs make such great police K-9s, sniffing out drugs at airports or during traffic stops.

Kevin opened the door, and the dogs were out like a shot. They loped around the pool and after a circle or two, tramped through his flowers, and then headed down the side yard. We followed and got to the edge of the house just as the dogs galloped through the open gate.

I looked at Kevin.

He shrugged his line-backer shoulders in denial. "I didn't leave it open."

If the dogs were running loose, there was an even better possibility they'd end up in doggie jail. I started after them, thanking my lucky stars I'd worn my running shoes instead of the really cute Marc Jacobs sandals I'd just bought. Still, Kevin got to the front of the house before I did.

I could see the dogs halfway up the street and took off after them. A landscape worker, or, I suppose in Ruby Point he would be called a "horticulturist," worked in one of the brick planters that lined the boulevard. Zeus and Tommy Boy were headed his way.

I yelled, "Stop those dogs."

He looked up.

"The dogs." I gestured so emphatically it's a wonder I didn't dislocate something.

He continued to stare.

Sheesh. How dense can you be?

Zeus and Tommy Boy ran up to him. Each grabbed a pant leg and held on.

He swung his shovel at them, narrowly missing the two furry heads.

Oh. No.

Zeus growled and adjusted his hold on the guy. Judging by the look on his face, dog teeth had reached flesh this time. He continued to swing the shovel.

Kevin was within earshot and used the commands we'd practiced.

"Zeus, Tommy Boy. Off."

The dogs released the worker, but looked disappointed. I didn't really blame them. I mean, seriously, what would you do if someone came after you with a shovel?

I finally caught up with them.

"Are you okay?"

"Are you an idiot?"

Kevin and I spoke in tandem. His was the voice of concern, mine the ill-mannered one.

Hey, I'm from Texas and we don't cotton to stupidity. Especially where it concerns our horses or our dogs.

The guy had crawled up onto the planter. Clearly not a dog person, and these were some big dogs. Okay, so maybe he'd reacted out of fear but still—a shovel?

Zeus and Tommy Boy sat at attention but continued to eye him with interest.

"Are you hurt?" I addressed the man but rested my hand on Tommy Boy's back. I could feel the tension in his body, but both dogs stayed in place.

The guy was young and wiry. His spiky black hair and multiple piercings suggested a latent punk-rocker look. The legs of his blue jeans were ripped, but I think they might have been before his encounter with Zeus and Tommy Boy. He jumped down from the planter and rubbed his leg.

"You need to keep your killer beasts under control." His dark eyes were hard and his posture tense.

If the dogs *had* actually broken skin and he went to the emergency room, it would definitely be the canine slammer.

"Well for cryin' in a bucket, let me take a look." I reached for his leg.

He jerked backward as if he thought I might bite, too.

"I'm fine." His voice was as tight as a fist.

Zeus and Tommy Boy both growled a deep rumble.

I looked at Kevin hoping he understood the seriousness of the situation. "Do you have a first-aid kit at your house?"

He nodded.

"Let's take the dogs home and I'll grab the kit." I turned to the gardener. "You sit and catch your breath. I'll be right back. Then we can take a look at your leg."

The guy continued to glare. With his dark, spikey hair, he kind of reminded me of one of those Texas horned lizards that puff up so they're all spiny when they're upset.

Kevin gave the command for the dogs to follow, and the four of us trouped back down the street toward his house. The dogs periodically glanced back as if to make sure the guy was staying put.

It took very little time for Kevin to find his first-aid kit and for me to head back to where we'd left Mister Angry Pants, but by the time I returned to the planter, the landscape worker was nowhere to be found.

What a fruitcake. I guess he must have been okay or he would've stuck around. Heading back to Kevin's to gather my things, I looked for one of the landscaping company's trucks, but didn't see a vehicle of any kind. On second thought, in such a fancy schmancy community they don't often leave the maintenance trucks out in plain sight. Maybe he'd needed to move on to another area of Ruby Point.

The morning had warmed up. I stopped back in at Kevin's and reminded him to keep up the behavior modification. I felt sure it would eventually work. Sometimes dogs can get into a barking cycle, and you have to break that cycle. I left with a promise to Kevin I'd check in tomorrow to see what kind of progress he'd made.

I pulled out of the drive and drove a short ways down the street to my friend, Diana's, house. Er, castle.

Diana's showcase abode dwarfed Kevin's, and her graceful flower-filled front entrance always made me think of the magic and glamour of a bygone era in Hollywood. The era that brought us stars like Elizabeth Taylor, Sophia Loren, Katherine Hepburn, and yes, Diana Knight.

You might recognize the name. Diana Knight had been a perky

heroine in a series of big-screen romantic comedies a few decades ago, and, though it turned out her leading man had been gay, the public still loved her. In fact, there had been a recent nostalgic resurgence of interest in her movies. She was still perky, at least in the personality sense.

In the physical sense, not so much.

Diana was a widow, I believe for the fourth time, having out-lived a college sweetheart, a fellow actor, a banker, and finally a business tycoon. She'd recently been keeping company with a local restaurateur, though she claimed it wasn't serious. She no longer acted but now used her considerable celebrity to advance her first love—rescue animals.

We'd met because Diana volunteered at the Laguna Beach Animal Rescue League, and I did, too. We were in the throes of planning the annual "Fur Ball" which was a "cough-up-some-cash" black-tie affair for the ARL. Diana had chaired the event for the past few years, and somehow this year I'd been roped into being her co-chair.

Being a co-chair with Diana meant there really wasn't much heavy lifting involved because she had it down to a fine science. She and I had spent a day last week calling corporate sponsors and setting up the advertising, which in most cases Diana'd been able to get comped. It was near impossible to tell this woman no.

Since I was in the area, I decided to drop off the final ad copy I'd picked up the day before from the graphic designer. I thought it had turned out great.

The picture was a handsome Doberman in a tux waltzing with a classy Siamese in a ball gown under a title that said: "Fur Ball—Cough Up Some Cash for the Laguna Beach ARL" and then gave all the details of the event. It was a picture the graphic designer had manipulated via magic software, you understand. I can assure you no animals were embarrassed in the making of this ad.

I was sure Diana would love it, but still this was her big event, and so I wanted to run it by her.

I rang the doorbell, and her housekeeper answered the door.

"Hello, Bella. Is Diana here?" I asked.

"No, I am sorry. She is not in at the moment. Can I give her a message?" The dark-haired beauty raised her soft musical voice to be heard over the cacophony of barking in the background.

Diana often took the more difficult rescue cases and at times had up to a dozen dogs in the house. Canine chaos.

"Bella, honey, I don't know how you do it." I patted her arm.

"Would you give her this, please?" I handed over the ad copy.

Bella took the folder and promised to see that Diana got it.

"Tell her I'll give her a call tomorrow."

Back in my car, I waved at the Ruby Point guard, and then left the gated community. I turned in the direction of Main Beach. Heading down Broadway, I made a quick stop at Whole Foods, and then pointed myself toward home.

My home is an eclectic blend of styles. It's nothing like my mama's house, which is always ready for a feature spread in *House Beautiful*. My house is hardly ever ready for its close-up. Not because I hadn't been raised right but because I basically didn't care about fancy things. It was clean, it was comfortable, it was mine.

I walked in and kicked off my shoes.

Dogbert, my rescue mixed-breed mutt, bounded across the room to greet me. He's part Spaniel, part Terrier, and parts unknown. He's the most adorable mutt alive.

Always faithful, always thrilled to see me. He is the love of my life.

I sat on the floor for some serious puppy hugs and flipped on the TV.

I have an incredible view of the Pacific out my patio doors and an open floor plan that takes full advantage of it. I'd paid a pretty price for my gorgeous view but I'd never regretted it.

Promising a long walk later, I gave Dog a final tummy rub and got to my feet. The television in my family room is visible from my kitchen, allowing me to monitor what's happening in the world as I prepare dinner. I use the term "prepare dinner" loosely.

I unpacked the organic mayonnaise I'd just purchased and opened a can of tuna. Sad, I know. Here I am within view of the ocean. You'd think I could get some fresh fish.

I was soon swarmed by Thelma and Louise, my two cats. I dumped half the tuna into a bowl and set it on the floor. Dogbert hurried over but was too late.

"None left for you, boy." I smiled at his resigned sigh. Upstaged by the felines again.

National news shifted to local news, and I listened for an update on the weather as I stirred some fresh cilantro and mayo into what was left of the tuna.

"Police are on the scene of what officers are calling an 'unexplained death' in the upscale gated community of Ruby Point."

That got my attention.

Not just Diana and Kevin but practically all of the residents of Ruby Point are clients or acquaintances of mine.

A female reporter, in a long-sleeved business suit that was much too warm for Southern California, and a hairdo that was much too big for this decade, gave the live report.

"The body was found this afternoon and police are at this time going door to door speaking to residents. Officers have not yet identified the individual, but the investigation centers around the house you see behind me."

I tried to see the home behind Big-Hair but couldn't quite make out the property. The homes in Ruby Point are all so different and individual that if I could get a glimpse I might recognized it, but I just couldn't see enough to tell.

The pounding on my door startled me. "Well, for cryin' in a bucket! I'm coming, and by the way I have a doorbell." I stomped to the door and yanked it open.

The doorway was filled with the poster boy for *People's* Sexiest Man Alive. I'm not often speechless, but short of asking if Christmas had come early, I was at a loss for words.

"Carolina Lamont?" His voice had a deep serious-as-a-heart-attack timbre.

"Yes."

"Detective Judd Malone."

Uh-oh. I was pretty sure this was about my earlier break-in. I wouldn't put it past Mel to call the police. But for the Laguna PD to send a detective? Really?

"Do you have identification?" I asked.

He hadn't offered a badge or an ID, and though I didn't truly think serial killers looked like Brad Pitt's brother and stalked pet therapists, you just can't be too careful.

He reached inside his jacket pocket and handed me a card.

Apparently business cards had replaced badges.

"May I come in?" He spoke awfully proper for a tough-guy detective but, hey, I'm from Texas so it always seems to me that folks are puttin' on airs.

I opened the door a bit further, and he shouldered past me.

Judd Malone smacked of attitude. He wore black jeans, a black leather jacket, and a chip on his shoulder. He scanned the room, his baby blues taking in my overstuffed couch, easy chairs, and crowded bookshelves. Thelma and Louise, perched in the windowsill, replete with tuna, each opened an eye and then, unimpressed, went back to their beauty sleep. Dogbert climbed from his doggie bed, trotted over for a sniff, but then also dismissed Malone and went back to his nap.

"Can I get you something to drink?" Some southern hospitality is automatic. Even when you have an unannounced guest. Even a guest who might arrest you. "Coffee, coke, iced tea?"

He shook his head and continued his scan.

"Well, then. What can I help you with, Detective Judd Malone?"

"I understand you visited Kevin Blackstone today?"

Okay, maybe not about the brooch. "Yes, I did. What about Kevin?"

I had a really bad feeling about this.

"Kevin Blackstone is dead."

Get Fluffy

Excerpt

"Colorful characters and a cheerfully compelling tone, all combined to make a mystery worth barking about."
—*Linda O. Johnson, author of* THE MORE THE TERRIER, *Berkley Prime Crime*

Get Fluffy
Book Two, The Pampered Pets Mysteries
By Sparkle Abbey

Yes, Melinda has been feuding with Mona, the queen of Laguna Beach's dog-loving divas. But Mel never expected Mona to end up murdered.

Mona loved Fluffy. No, Mona worshipped Fluffy. She'd never abandon her dog.

Something was wrong. Why would Mona leave her front door unlocked, the alarm off, and her cell phone behind?

Fluffy shoved me out of the way and trotted down the hallway to the next room.

I'd barely turned the knob when Fluffy barged past me, head-butting the door against the wall with a loud bang.

I stumbled through the doorway. It wasn't a room. It was a mini-palace fit for a movie star. Fluffy's palace. A white sheepskin rug in front of her personal fireplace, a king-sized sleigh bed, and a dressing screen (why a dog needed a dressing screen was beyond me). Fresh filtered water dripped into her Wedgewood doggie bowl.

It was also a disaster.

Fluffy's wardrobe was strewn throughout the room, draped precariously on the bed, and hanging out of open drawers. While Mona had an obscene amount of photos, Fluffy had her own slew of trophies and ribbons. All of them haphazardly tossed about.

The room looked like it had been ransacked.

Fluffy disappeared behind the disheveled bed. Her tail stopped wagging, and she whined softly.

That's when I saw her.

At first, I wasn't certain what I was looking at. Then it became clear. Mona was sprawled on the floor as if posing for a men's magazine. It was almost picture perfect, except for the blood matting her five-hundred-dollar haircut and the gold statue stuck in her head.

I hesitantly moved closer. Fluffy nuzzled Mona's cheek. When she didn't move, Fluffy pawed her shoulder, still whining.

"I don't think she's getting up, girl," I said softly.

Mona was deader than a stuffed Poodle.

Chapter One

I am nothing like my cousin, Caro, the "pet shrink."

She's a redhead, I'm a brunette. She's kept her Texas twang, I busted my butt to lose mine (except when I'm honked off, then my southern drawl can strike like a Gulf coast hurricane). She's calm and direct. I'm equally direct. As for calm, I have to admit, sometimes my emotions tend to overrule my better judgment.

So who would have thought I'd end up in the middle of a Laguna Beach murder investigation, just like Caro?

From my very first breath, Mama had groomed me to be Miss America, just like her and her sister, Katherine. Or a Dallas Cowboy Cheerleader, which in Texas was the more prestigious of the two. By my twenty-first birthday, I'd gathered ten first-place pageant crowns like Fourth of July parade candy. That's when my beauty queen career had been dethroned in public scandal.

Everyone believed she "encouraged" a male judge to cast his vote for me. As for what I thought, well, no daughter wants to believe her mama is a hustler. To this day, Mama still won't talk about *The Incident* above a whisper.

With the battle for the top crown over, I'd traded in my tiaras, sashes, and hair spray for Swarovski crystal collars, cashmere dog sweaters, and botanical flea dip. I left Texas and moved to Laguna Beach, California, a community known for its art, wealth, and love of dogs. I opened Bow Wow Boutique and catered to the canine who had everything.

I loved Laguna. Loved running my own business. I even loved the quirky folks whose lives revolved around their pooches. But sometimes I longed for Texas—wide open spaces, cowboy boots, and big-big hair. Who wouldn't?

It was mid-October. The tourists had packed up and headed home. The locals ventured out of their gated communities to enjoy all the beachside town had to offer. Most importantly, there was available parking downtown. At least until next May.

The annual Fur Ball had finally arrived—a community event to raise money for the Laguna Beach Animal Rescue League. The balmy weather was perfect for an outdoor fund-raiser.

As always at these shindigs, the humans coughed up large chunks of dough for a worthy cause. Breezy air kisses and alcohol flowed freely, while we all pretended to be best friends. Trust me, we were one society catfight away from a hell of an entertaining evening.

I looked down at Missy, my English Bulldog, who waited patiently at my feet. Her crystal-studded tiara sat lopsided on the top of her head, and a small puddle of drool had collected between her paws.

I straightened her crown and whispered, "We're up, girl. Let's show them what we've got."

With our heads held high, Missy and I strutted our stuff down the red carpet. The pup-a-razzi cameras flashed, and the crowd cheered. One reporter asked who'd made my strapless leather gown (Michael Kors), and another wanted to know how Missy had won her tiara (she'd placed first in Laguna Beach's Ugliest Bulldog contest last year).

Once we reached the end of the walkway, I leaned down to dab the drool from Missy's chin. "You did great." I kissed the top of her head. "Let's go find our friends."

Missy gave my hand a slobbery kiss, and then we made our way into the main event. Under an extravagant white tent and glittering lights, two hundred wealthy dog lovers and their four-legged friends paraded around in designer rags; both human and canine dripped with diamonds.

I quickly spotted Kimber Shores and her pug Noodles making their way in our direction. Kimber oozed understated glamour in her mauve jumpsuit. She'd definitely make Laguna's Best-Dressed List.

"Mel, I'm so glad I found you," she declared.

As we air-kissed, the low-cut back of her outfit offered a glimpse of her many tattoos.

"Noodles looks amazing," she continued in her melodious voice. "I'm so glad you talked me out of the velvet jacket."

Kimber and her pug had stopped by the shop earlier. Noodles had been in desperate need of a wardrobe update. I'd managed to wrangle him out of his Hugh Hefner smoking jacket and into a modest white tux and tails. Noodles sat in front of Missy, his marble eyes watching the slobber slide down the corners of her mouth.

I smiled affectionately. "He really isn't a velvet kinda guy. I love the top hat. Nice choice."

Out of the corner of my eye I could see Grey Donovan, my fiancé of two years, heading in our direction. Kimber must have noticed, too; she immediately looked uncomfortable.

To the outside world, Grey's and my relationship was seen as a tad unorthodox. We were the on-again-off-again type. Presently, we were "on."

"Ah, I see you're not alone. Anyway, I just wanted to say thanks." She grabbed my hand and squeezed.

"You're welcome. Stop by Bow Wow when you get a chance. I have the perfect sweater-vest for Noodles."

Kimber and her pug disappeared into the crowd just as Grey arrived.

"Caro and Diana organized a great event." He handed me a glass of pinot noir. He looked amazing in his black tux. But then, he always looked good.

Missy sniffed his pant leg, double-checking he hadn't stepped out on her. He bent down and gave her some love. She snorted happily, lapping up Grey's affection. I knew exactly how she felt.

I took a sip of wine, appreciating the black-pepper finish. I snagged us each a tomato and goat cheese tart from a passing waiter (he was out of pigs-in-a-blanket, Missy's favorite).

"I hate to break it to you, but it's the Dallas upbringing. Every society girl knows how to throw a successful charity fund-raiser by her eighteenth birthday." I took a bite of the tart and sighed. Delicious. "But you're right. It's a fabulous evening."

Grey, an undercover FBI agent, worked white-collar crime— mostly art theft. He could be gone for two days or two months without a whisper of his well-being. I never knew if he was sipping espresso in Paris or being held hostage in a deserted warehouse in East LA.

His decision to keep me completely in the dark of his activities— his way of protecting me—had finally pushed me to the breaking point. I'd realized if I had trouble *dating* Grey, our marriage could end up a disaster. So I'd called off the wedding (two months before the big day), causing a swirl of rumors and speculation.

I swear, I'd tried to return the six-carat sapphire engagement ring that had belonged to his great-grandmother, but Grey had refused to accept it. He believed we could work it out. I really wanted him to be right.

"To Caro and Diana. May the evening continue to be a howling success." Grey lifted his glass, and I followed suit.

We mingled with the other guests and made our way to the table of auction items. I spotted my cousin next to the open bar, schmoozing with a celebrity dog trainer who currently judged a TV reality pet show. I didn't have to hear her southern drawl to know she'd used it to her advantage.

She fooled a lot of people at first glance. She looked as soft as a hothouse wildflower, but inside she was all iron and grit.

At the moment, Caro and I weren't exactly speaking. Since our childhood, Caro had always saved something or someone. A few years ago that had included her ex-husband who deserved to rot behind prison walls instead.

To this day, she continued to analyze how her marriage had fallen apart. I'd expressed my opinion (truth be told, it was unsolicited at the time, but that hadn't stopped me), and Caro got her feelings hurt. We had *words*.

I know I'm the one who should apologize first, but, knowing me, my smartass mouth would probably make matters worse. Sometimes I'm better with dogs than people.

Recently, I'd broken my vow of silence. Caro's best friend, Diana Knight, a former movie star and one of Laguna's resident celebrities, had been arrested for murder. In my experience, who better to deliver bad news than family?

Luckily for Diana, she was one of Caro's success stories. Caro had helped clear Diana of a bogus murder wrap and in the process had almost gotten herself killed. Thankfully, the police—and her quick thinking—had saved her.

A slow smile tugged the corners of my mouth as I waited for my cousin to turn in my direction.

Competition runs deep in the Montgomery blood, our mothers' side of the family tree. Over the years, Caro had managed to intermittently suppress her competitiveness. I, on the other hand, let mine run free. Electrified with the sudden possibility of getting the best of my cousin, I grabbed Grey's arm. "Let's go say hi to Caro."

"No." He didn't even take his eye off the list of silent auction items.

"Come on. You just said she did a great job."

"I'm not going to be a vehicle for you to flaunt that thing." He flicked his auction list toward the gaudy, but sentimental, brooch pinned strategically to my gown.

The pin was a family heirloom, a twenty-two karat gold basket filled with fruit made of precious gems. Rubies, diamonds, emeralds, and topaz. You'd never know by looking at the garish thing that it was insured for more money than all four years of my Stanford College tuition.

I adjusted the brooch. "It gives my little black dress something extra."

Grey's green eyes softened. His gaze traveled from the bottom of my floor-length, strapless, leather gown and ended at the gaudy heirloom.

I felt the heat flood my checks and pretended his blatant appraisal didn't make my knees weak.

"*Little* is one description. Leave your cousin alone," he said on a sigh.

Poor Grey. He was my fiancé, but he was also Caro's friend.

"Grandma Tillie left the pin to me. I only retrieved what was rightfully mine." Grandma was very specific in her will. The brooch was to go to her "*favorite* granddaughter." That was me. Then again, Caro was just as convinced it was her.

"You broke into Caro's house and stole it," he said.

"Only after she'd marched into Bow Wow Boutique, in the middle of the day, and stole it from my purse in front of God and my customers."

He looked at me as if I'd lost my mind. "So that makes breaking into her private safe okay?"

I grimaced. There was a tingle of regret about my actions that day. It had taken a few tries to figure out the combination, but I had.

Caro hadn't used an easy-to-hack combination. No. She'd used something much more personal that only I could truly understand the significance of.

When I thought about that, I felt like a traitor who deserved to be shot at twenty paces. So, I tried not to think about it.

I was sure I'd pay for my transgression at some point.

"Mel, do you want the brooch, or to make Carolina squirm?" Grey asked.

"Is there a right or wrong answer?"

"Yes."

I took another sip of wine, letting the warmth from the alcohol seep through me. I know it's selfish, but I wanted both. Hey, at least I'm honest.

Caro finally turned and caught my eye. I held back the urge to jump up and down. Instead, I lifted my wine glass in salute, making sure she could see I had on the brooch.

She hesitated for a second, aware we were gossip prey. Like the southern lady she was, she returned the salute with an amused smile. We both knew she was plotting revenge. *Game on, cousin.* I'd have to find a better hiding place than my cookie jar.

Grey shook his head in defeat and directed my attention to the banquet tables of donated items for the silent auction. There was one item that had me seriously contemplating going home for my credit card. An African safari. I sighed, knowing I was about to spend too much money, and I wasn't even buzzed.

"You're doing the right thing," Grey said.

"I've always wanted to go on an African safari."

"I was talking about Caro."

"I do have some self-control." I set my glass on the table and adjusted his bow tie. Not because it needed it. But because it was our first public appearance since the almost-wedding.

"I just wanted her to see I had it," I explained.

"I don't always understand you two. Or why your friends encourage your harebrained competition."

I retrieved my glass with a shrug. "Because it's harmless fun."

I scribbled an obscene dollar amount alongside my bidding number on the safari listing, knowing I'd bumped the mayor out of the playing field.

Grey whistled softly. "Playing to win?"

"Why else would I play?"

"If I could have your attention," Amelia Hudges, the ARL director, spoke into the microphone.

Everyone turned expectantly in Amelia's direction. I almost choked on my wine. Amelia looked like an over-the-top Bette Midler with her frizzed-out orange hair and heavily beaded gown. *Good God.* Had someone died and covered the mirrors in her house?

"We've made some quick calculations after a few passes around the room." She paced the stage in excitement. "Due to your generosity, the silent auction has already grossed an estimated two hundred fifty thousand dollars." Amelia's high-pitched twitter competed with resounding applause and excited barking.

"Now it's time to get serious." She raised a freckled hand for silence. "We're more than halfway to our goal of three hundred fifty thousand dollars. Listen to your heart, not your accountant. Open your wallets, and let's start the live auction! Find your seats, everyone."

Grey, Missy, and I ping-ponged through the noisy crowd and were the last of our group to arrive. We were about to sit when Tova Randall, a highly successful lingerie model who had just moved to town, called out my name.

Everyone at our table watched as Tova bounced closer. It wasn't her perfect pale complexion or her luxurious auburn hair that drew our attention. It was her blush-pink, silk-taffeta gown hugging her famous curves. Those same curves had paid for her thirteen-million-dollar home in the hills, down the street from Grey's place.

"Melinda Langston, you owe me fifteen hundred dollars," she announced in a not-so-conversational tone.

"I beg your pardon?"

She was drunk. It was the only plausible explanation. I looked at our tablemates and shook my head apologetically.

Unlike Tova, her Yorkiepoo loved me. And I loved Kiki in return. Her pink, mini-taffeta dress rustled as her tiny five-pound body wiggled in excitement. I reached down to pet the adorable dog. Kiki immediately rewarded me with enthusiastic kisses.

Missy sniffed Tova's pocket puppy in the universal dog greeting. Unimpressed, Missy crawled under the table, looking for a spot to nap.

Tova gripped the diamond-encrusted leash tighter, pulling Kiki closer to her. "You gave my baby fleas," she huffed.

Hell's bells. What was she talking about?

Chapter Two

A loud murmur rippled over our table. All eyes were on us, waiting for my reaction to Tova's outrageous claim.

I set my half-empty glass of pinot noir next to my plate. "I don't know what you're talking about."

Tova lifted her chin higher. "Kiki and I got kicked out of Mommy and Doggie Yoga because she had fleas."

Seriously, how was that my fault? Besides, it wasn't the end of the world. It happens to the best of dogs (although Missy's never been afflicted with them). I'm sure even Rin Tin Tin had a case of fleas. Once.

"That must have been embarrassing for you," I said to the crazy lady.

Tova sucked in her cheeks, producing a well-practiced pout. "She obviously got them from Bow Wow."

What the—? I leaned forward, invading her personal bubble. She stepped back and had the presence of mind to look worried. "I don't think so. Have you considered she caught them from a dog at yoga?" I kept my tone sweet and non-confrontational.

A glance at Grey told me I wasn't as successful as I'd thought.

He cleared his throat. "Ladies, can't this wait?"

Tova picked up Kiki and pressed her wiggly body against her not-so-natural cleavage. "I was assured it didn't happen there."

I was assured it didn't happen there, I mimicked silently. "Well, I just assured you it didn't happen at Bow Wow."

By now we had an audience. Not just our small table of people. Oh no, half the room leaned in our direction, waiting for me to knock Tova on her beautiful butt.

I walked a fine line. Fleas aren't deadly, but no one would knowingly expose their pet or themselves. I clenched and unclenched my fists. What to do, what to do . . . ?

"Melinda, what's going on?" Mona Michaels and her Afghan Hound, Fluffy, paraded to our table.

Great. Trouble on six legs.

Mona ruled the rich and famous of Laguna Beach with the wave of her aristocratic hand and her elite American Express Black Card. She had her plastic surgeon on speed dial, injectable Botox in her purse, and her private chef on a short leash.

Her simple black Valentino gown was most likely the envy of every woman at the ball. She was what the gated community housewives dreamed of being when they grew up.

Unfortunately for me, Mona and my mother were childhood friends. Mona thought that meant she could dictate, and I'd blindly follow. Not likely. I wasn't a Mona fan.

From behind, Fluffy looked exactly like her human. A mistake I'd made more than once. *Awkward.*

Tonight, Fluffy seemed more haughty than normal. Her jeweled collar with a diamond-crusted, heart-shaped pendant sparkled like a mirror ball, and I'm guessing was equally as heavy. She looked like she couldn't be bothered mingling with us average humans.

Too bad Mona didn't feel the same indifference. She narrowed her assessing blue eyes at me and waited for an explanation.

Why she thought she'd get one was beyond me.

"Go back to your posse, Mona. Everything here's just hunky-dory."

Mona motioned to the crowd; her shocking white hair flowed softly around her razor-sharp cheekbones. "It is plain to everyone you do *not* have this situation under control, otherwise Amelia wouldn't be cowering in the corner of the stage waiting for you to finish."

As always, Mona's condescending clipped voice raised my hackles.

"You may want to consider keeping your voice down," Grey warned under his breath.

Too late. All eyes had followed Mona. Once she'd insinuated herself into my business, I had my reputation to protect. I turned my attention back to Tova.

"You still haven't explained why I owe you money?"

"Well, I had to get Kiki groomed," Tova stammered. Mona's presence loomed over us, and Tova was beginning to crack. Amateur. If she wanted to make it here, she'd have to develop a thicker skin.

"And?" I could feel the weight of the room shift towards us waiting to hear the answer. Who knew dogs could be so quiet?

"My lawyer says you have to reimburse me for it."

"Oh, hell no."

Murmurs rolled through the room like Main Beach waves crashing against the rocks.

Tova stood her ground. "She got them while on your property. You have to pay," she insisted.

I hiked up my gown, which pooled around my three-inch heels. I wished I was wearing my motorcycle boots. "You're the only one with fleas." I took a breath and tried to control my rising voice and cover the Texas accent that was threatening to make an appearance. "If this was a Bow Wow issue, someone else would have said something."

"They're afraid of you," Tova whined.

"You're ridiculous," Mona pronounced with the wave of her hand.

"You're out of control," I said at the same time.

I don't know if Mona was talking to me or Tova. I was talking about both of them.

Tova shook her head. "You don't know what kind of nightmare I've been through. Kiki's wardrobe had to be dry-cleaned, my carpet steamed, her travel bag replaced, and she had to be groomed a second time after her botanical dip."

I'd had enough. "I do not have fleas!" I turned to the room, hands on hips and asked, "Did I give any of you fleas?"

There was a lot of throat-clearing and minimal eye contact. No one said a word. It would have been comical if I hadn't been so honked off.

I narrowed my eyes on Tova. "Looks like it's just you."

"Enough." Mona pointed at Tova. "Take your dog and sit."

"This isn't over." Tova looked between Mona and me like a confused puppy; her shoulders sagged, and her bottom lip quivered slightly. "You'll regret pushing me around."

"Does this mean you and Kiki won't be by tomorrow to pick up the barrettes you special-ordered?"

"Melinda," Mona said, "If you know what's good for you, you'll sit and stop causing a scene."

"Don't. As much as you like to worm your way into my life, and everyone else's for that matter, you're not my mother."

Mona turned toward me. A glint of fire danced in her eyes. A chill of warning rolled down my back.

"True," she said. "Fluffy *earned* her crown. I didn't need to act like a dog in heat for the judges to see her true *talent*."

That was it. The woman insulted me and my Mama.

Bitter emotion churned until it turned into a roar of fury. I yanked my wine glass from the table and tossed the deep ruby contents on Mona's dress. Immediately, I knew I'd crossed the line. The fat was in the fire now.

Grey groaned in disappointment. Missy jumped out from under the table and barked, her crown rolling under my chair.

Everyone else was deathly silent.

Mona stood frozen, her hands in the air.

Then suddenly she hissed. "You fool."

Fluffy tossed her pale tresses from her eyes and snarled.

The room erupted into chaos. People jumped up from their seats. They talked over each other, shocked, yet lapping up the juicy gossip of my behavior.

The dogs barked, Missy included. Canines turned on each other and their humans. Leashes wrapped around chairs, tables, and human legs, dragging everything behind them in their excitement.

"Don't touch me," Mona ordered to a handful of dimwits who thought they'd get into her good graces by mopping the wine from her dress.

I dropped to my knees to retrieve Missy's crown.

"If you'd like to use the ladies' room, I'd be happy to keep an eye on Fluffy," Grey offered, his calm voice sounding out-of-place amidst the pandemonium.

I got to my feet, Missy's leash in one hand, her crown in the other.

Mona yanked the white cloth napkin Grey held out for her. She patted her dress as if taking a public wine bath was an everyday occurrence. "If you don't leave now, I'll call the police and have you arrested." She quickly found her normal condescending voice.

I couldn't believe what I was hearing. "Are you kidding me? You deserved it. Everyone knows it." I gestured toward the group of gawkers.

"Melinda, you've done enough." Grey's tone was tense and didn't hold room for disagreement.

I whipped around. "You're taking her side?" I felt like I'd been stabbed in the heart.

"No, I'm trying to keep you from going to jail," he muttered.

I snagged my gold clutch from the table and shoved Missy's crown on my head. Tears burned my eyes. "I'm sorry I've embarrassed you."

I meant it. I was sorry. Of course, that didn't change the fact that

I'd just acted like an idiot. My snap judgment was in full throttle. Once in gear, it was difficult to apply the brakes.

He grabbed my arm and stopped my dramatic exit. "This isn't about me." He jerked his head toward the back of the room.

Caro looked like I'd just kicked her dog, Dogbert. Her face had turned the same color as the vintage red satin gown she wore. Her tightened lips formed a straight line, and her snappy green eyes had narrowed into angry slits. Sam Gallanos, her date, stood silently at her side, his dark eyes studying me.

I'd forgotten all about Caro. I'd blindly embraced my anger and had completely lost sight of the fundraising goal for the Fur Ball.

Intense self-reproach latched onto my heart and squeezed. I wish I could say it was an unfamiliar feeling. But I couldn't.

I guided Missy through the mayhem with only one purpose in mind—to confront the only thing standing between me and a hasty exit so I could berate my lack of judgment in private.

"I didn't plan on making a scene," I said to my cousin. It was as close to an apology as I could manage at the moment.

Caro eyed the crown. Then the brooch.

Anyone else would have looked away and ignored me, casting me to social purgatory. Instead, her eyes locked onto mine, and she said, "You never do, sugar."

I couldn't argue. I'd left her one hell of a mess to clean up.

"You'll need to call Nigel," Caro's soft southern accent hung on the family lawyer's name.

I covered the brooch protectively with my hand.

"Are you fixin' to sue me, cousin?" I asked, unable to keep the Texas out of my voice.

She shook her head and looked at me like I'd hopped on the crazy train, which apparently I had.

"Geeze Louise, Mel. You just humiliated Mona in public. You know she won't let you get away with it."

Caro's Easy Peasy Peanut Butter, Parsley & Banana Dog Treats

Ingredients

1 banana
1 cup oat flour
2/3 cup rolled oats
1/2 cup dried parsley
3 tablespoons peanut butter
1 egg

Instructions

Preheat oven to 300° F

Mash the banana, add the other ingredients. Set the mixture aside for a little while, five minutes or so. Then roll the dough into balls. The size should be adjusted for the size of your dog. Press the balls into flat "cookies" and place on a cookie sheet. Bake for about 45 minutes or until golden brown. Set aside to cool.

You can store the treats in the refrigerator or freeze them to be used later. You'll need to unthaw a bit before sharing in order to protect your dog's teeth.

These also make great gifts, and they're gluten-free for pooches who are on a gluten-restricted diet. Also, the parsley is great for your dog's breath. Enjoy!

Acknowledgements

First we'd like to thank those who shared their Greyhound experiences, especially Jennifer Stich and John Martin. Your stories enriched *Fifty Shades of Greyhound*, and your willingness to answer our many questions and share stories about Ollie & Elvis made us love the breed even more. We very much appreciate your time, and we know your rescues are glad to have found you.

To the Greyhound rescue groups such as GreySave Greyhound Adoption, Nebraska Italian Greyhound Rescue, Heartland Greyhound Adoption, and many others out there doing such important work, we say thank you on behalf of those you save.

We continue to be amazed by the fabulous team at Bell Bridge Books. Your editorial support, your marketing savvy, and your belief in us as writers, is awesome. And your willingness to listen to one more crazy idea makes you beyond awesome. Thank you.

Christine Witthohm, our agent, at Book Cents Literary Agency, in short, you rock.

We also owe an enormous debt of appreciation to our families who give us not only the time to write but also the confidence to keep going; and who put up with dinner conversations that include plotting new ways to kill people.

Christine, Cindy, Tami, your love and support mean the world, and your constructive critique makes us better writers.

And last, but by no means least, a huge thank-you to our readers. Your love of Caro and Mel and their stories are why we write. We love to hear from you. Please sign up for our newsletter, follow us on Facebook, Twitter, Pinterest, and Goodreads, and keep those emails coming!

Mary Lee and Anita, aka Sparkle Abbey

SparkleAbbey.com

About the Authors

Sparkle Abbey is the pseudonym of two mystery authors (Mary Lee Woods and Anita Carter). They are friends and neighbors as well as co-writers of the Pampered Pets Mystery Series. The pen name was created by combining the names of their rescue pets—Sparkle (Mary Lee's cat) and Abbey (Anita's dog). They reside in central Iowa, but if they could write anywhere, you would find them on the beach with their laptops and, depending on the time of day, with either an iced tea or a margarita.

Mary Lee

Mary Lee Salsbury Woods is the "Sparkle" half of Sparkle Abbey. She is past-president of Sisters in Crime—Iowa and a member of Mystery Writers of America, Romance Writers of America, Kiss of Death, the RWA Mystery Suspense Chapter, Sisters in Crime, and the SinC internet group Guppies.

Prior to publishing the Pampered Pets Mystery Series with Bell Bridge Books, Mary Lee won first place in the Daphne du Maurier contest, sponsored by the Kiss of Death chapter of RWA, and was a finalist in Murder in the Grove's mystery contest, as well as Killer Nashville's Claymore Dagger contest.

Mary Lee is an avid reader and supporter of public libraries. She lives in Central Iowa with her husband, Tim, and Sparkle, the rescue cat namesake of Sparkle Abbey. In her day job, she is the non-techie in the IT Department. Any spare time she spends reading and enjoying her sons and daughter-in-laws, and four grandchildren.

Anita

Anita Carter is the "Abbey" half of Sparkle Abbey. She is a member of Sisters in Crime—Iowa, and a member of Mystery Writers of America, Romance Writers of America, Kiss of Death, the RWA Mystery Suspense chapter, and Sisters in Crime.

She grew up reading Trixie Belden, Nancy Drew, and the Margo Mystery series by Jerry B. Jenkins (years before his popular *Left Behind* Series.) Her family is grateful all the years of "fending for yourself" dinners of spaghetti and frozen pizza have finally paid off, even though they haven't exactly stopped.

In Anita's day job, she works for a staffing company. She also lives in Central Iowa with her husband and four children, son-in-law, grandchild, and two rescue dogs, Chewy and Sophie.

CPSIA information can be obtained at www.ICGtesting.com
Printed in the USA
LVOW07s1329310315

432736LV00005B/145/P